Slipp In Tim

A Lord Thyme-Slipp Adventure

Jonas Lane

To Lily
Best wishos
Jonas Lane

Published by JAC Books, 2017.

Slipp In Time

Jonas Lane

First published. March 13, 2017

Copyright © 2003, 2017 JONAS LANE.

Written by JONAS LANE.

A JAC BOOK, published by JAC Books.

Contents

Slipp In Time

About the author

Jonas Lane is the author's pen name, an anagram of his real one, due to the following:

a) His real name is way too common.

b) No one would read his books if he'd used his Jedi or Elvish name.

c) Jon A Slane, Jona Slane and Lana Ensoj don't sound as cool.

d) He's rubbish at cryptic anagrams.

His passion for writing and entertaining helps when trying to capture the hearts and minds of the children that he teaches. In return, they inspire him with their laughter and enthusiasm.

Having picked up his pen in anger once more, he hopes his over-active imagination, daft sense of humour and a mind that's a mine of useless information will encourage others to follow the writing path he's neglected to travel himself for too long.

Jonas lives with his wife, dog and hyper-activeness in a village far, far away...

Visit Jonas at his website www.jonaslaneauthor.com

For Alex,

About the boy that he was,
For the man that he's become.

Chapter 1 – Saturday Morning Fever!

Codswallop. Founded in 896 AD by the Saxon Chief Cod. Whilst leading his family and tribe of settlers across England, Cod fell from his horse, fast asleep, landing next to a small river, (the fall failing to wake him from his slumber!) Knowing what a temper he possessed if woken, the settlers made camp for the night, waiting for their leader to arise. They hoped that he would awake in a far better mood than he had shown during their travels, ready to continue their journey to a new home on the east coast. But Cod the Lazy, as he became known, couldn't be bothered to travel any further. So, he decided to start his settlement here, on the banks of the Skally River that flowed gently down the forested hills to the sea. Due to this legendary laziness, Codswallop never developed in the way of other Saxon settlements of that time!

Codswallop, where the population is thought to be about 792 people. Roughly. There may be more living in and around the village, were it not for the locals following in their famous founder's footsteps. Not even being bothered enough to fill in their last census form!

Codswallop. Most famous for being the home of the Blinkingshire Wallop. A large suet pudding made for farmers who were out working in the fields all day during the 19th century. This rare dish consists of bacon, eggs, cheese, pickle, rhubarb and custard. Breakfast. Lunch. Pudding. All mixed together to become one giant Wallop! (It's fair to say that this local dish has not gone down in history as famously as the Cornish pasty!)

Codswallop, probably the most boring village in England. No, Britain. No, the whole world. Probably. Nothing ever really happened here. No, really, I mean nothing EVER happens. No invasions, robberies, mysteries, adventures. No dastardly deeds or infamous events. Nothing.

At least none that Alex McClellan knew about growing up in the picturesque, but sleepy little village, nestled in the hills overlooking the quaint, windy cobbled streets of Skallywag Bay. It was difficult for any child growing up in Codswallop, especially with the nearest major town being over twenty miles away. But it was even harder for a ten-year-old boy like Alex. A ten-year-old with an over-active imagination, a thirst for excitement and adventure, fuelled by hours with his nose in a book. Or by watching video clips and films on the internet about the wonders of the wider world. (That's when reception was good enough in the village to stream it of course!)

The only good thing about the village was the fact that his cousin, Georgina, lived there too.

Georgie, as she prefers to be known, was eighteen months older than Alex, as she constantly reminded him, wearing the fact like a badge of honour to win any argument or disagreement between them. But, usually, Alex looked up to her like a big sister. In fact, they were so close and looked so similar that most people thought they were siblings, which they played on, especially with both being an only child. Neither had ever really wanted a brother or sister, so now they had the best of both worlds, spending as much time together as they wanted to. But still being able to send the other one home when they'd had enough of each other!

Usually, they were round one or another's house anyway, playing, arguing, laughing, causing mischief and generally wondering if, or when, something exciting was going to happen to them.   But, as a rule, they often ended up disappointed. No, they always ended up disappointed.

That was until one fateful Saturday morning, early last autumn.   Little did they know that from that day, their lives would never be the same again…

"Hi Auntie Flora, is Georgie coming out to play today?" Alex asked cheerfully as he stood on the doorstep of his cousin's house. "Mum's going shopping in Garnham and Dad's at the 'Space Wars' convention all day. Normally I'd have gone with him, but he's painted himself blue, like one of the characters from Revenge of the Banzai! Plus, he's meeting his best mate Bob, so it's a bit too geeky for me this time!"

His Auntie Flora, a huge, hairy, forbidding woman, leant on the doorframe in front of him chuckling, a large, half-eaten sandwich wedged between the fingers of her chubby left hand.

 "I can see that might put you off going!" She laughed loudly, continuing, "But, pet, Georgie won't be free to play just yet. She's starting a paper round today."

Alex frowned. "A paper round? Why on earth is she doing that?" Where work was concerned, Georgie was one of the laziest people he knew, much in keeping with her fellow Codswallopians, as the locals are commonly known!

"Because my stingy Mum and Dad say that I can't have any more Pantora

Alphabeat charms for my bracelet unless I buy them myself!" A voice called from the hall behind Flora. There, Georgie stood, her long blonde hair tied tightly back, with a bright yellow cloth sack, twice the size of her, slung over a shoulder. "I'm up to Spawny, the DJ charm. That means that I have to do every Saturday for the next two years plus just to complete my collection!" Auntie Flora smiled again, exposing a small piece of lettuce stuck between two yellow front teeth as she spoke. "I think that you are exaggerating a little bit there dear. Anyway, you could always trade in your EYE-TAPP phone to make your money go a little further." She said.

Alex found the lettuce strangely hypnotic as it vibrated up and down in her mouth as she spoke. Was that a caterpillar in there too trying to make an escape? Urgh! He hoped not as the poor thing stood no real chance of survival!

"No way!" Georgie looked horrified! "It's bad enough living in this village, let alone not having a mobile phone! And I am so not exaggerating! You said yourself that because Dad's business hasn't as much work as it normally does, that we would have to be a bit more careful with our money and when I said, 'Ok as long as I've got my phone and could keep collecting my charms', you said 'Ok', as long as I saved for them from my pocket money I could have them, but when I worked it out that by saving a couple of quid a week it would take fifteen weeks to save for the next charm and as there are eight charms still to collect…" (Alex had forgotten how much Georgie could talk when she wanted to). "…That it would take me over two years to finish the set, by which time I would be a teenager and probably more interested in make-up and boys than jewellery. Plus, I've have to have the latest apps on my phone and…"

"Yes, yes I know. But we did say that if you got a little job too, we would help make up the difference." Georgie frowned as she tried to squeeze past her mother's huge doorstop of a bottom with the yellow sack.

"It's still not fair! I get to miss all the omnibus editions of my favourite programmes on a Saturday morning, like Rawdy Shores and Jollyfolks! It will take ages to deliver all these!" She moaned, pointing to the contents of the paper sack.

"Not if your lovely cousin helps you! Now, you wouldn't mind helping Georgie, would you Alex?" Asked Auntie Flora. Alex looked stunned. Let me see, he thought, walking around the village, delivering papers or lazing on the couch, watching TV, playing computer games, eating sweets? Decisions, decisions, decisions!

"I'd love to Flora, but I, er, promised Mum that I, er, would, er, help her, er, wash the, er, dog!" He lied, badly.

"When did you get a dog?" Georgie questioned. Drat! A small flaw in an otherwise brilliant excuse!

"I, er, didn't mean *THE* dog, meaning, er, a dog of our own. I meant A DOG, as it's, erm, National Dog Washing Day. YES! Yes, that's it, today's the day that you must find a dog that doesn't belong to you and wash it for charity and, er, ah…" He was now struggling to finish the lie that he so had fantastically created. "Anyway, why would I want to deliver papers without being paid for it?" He asked, changing the subject quickly.

Auntie Flora grinned suspiciously, as a bit of celery floated juicily around her gums. (Or was that mashed up caterpillar?)

"If you help my little angel, I'll make you one of those delicious home-made pies of mine that you love so very much." At the very thought of sampling

Flora's cooking, Alex was play-doh in her hands! Whilst Georgie was motivated by money and getting her own way, there was a much simpler way to Alex's heart. Through his stomach!

Flora was an amazing cook and, being the school dinner lady, could just about cook anything you asked her to, it always turning out delicious. However, her pastries, as well as her sweet and savoury pies, were just to die for! So, before he'd even realised it, Alex had said "Okay" and was pushing Georgie's bike, complete with paper sack, along the lane that led towards the village green.

Alex puffed and panted heavily, like an old steam train, as he wheeled the bike along, Georgie only holding the paper or magazine that next needed delivering.

"Hey, why am I am doing all the hard work?" Alex asked as they reached Mrs Patel's' cottage.

Georgie looked at him, shook her head and sighed. "Because I need to concentrate on delivering all the right papers to all the right houses. And besides," she continued, fluttering her eyes at him, "it's such a heavy sack and I am just a puny ickle girl! Boys are supposed to be so much tougher and stronger, aren't they? You're always saying so!"

"Well, yes, I suppose, but..."

"Good, I am glad you agree, so no need for you to moan then, is there?" Georgie said triumphantly as she went to post the latest copy of Mole Watchers Monthly through the letterbox of the small, pink, thatched cottage. Once again, Alex knew that he had been conned by his cousin, but he couldn't quite work out how to stop her. As he pondered how to prevent this from happening again, the two of them fairly zipped through delivering the rest of the paper round, with only a couple of minor mishaps along the way.

The first one came when Georgie was pinned down and licked like a giant lollipop by Baxter, the giant chocolate Labrador who lived at No.14 Penny Lane. He came bounding across the garden and launched himself at her as soon as she had opened the front gate.

"Get him off me!" Georgie yelled, Baxter's tongue covering her face like a gigantic sponge!

It took Mr Lancaster, his owner, and Alex five minutes to persuade Baxter that she was now totally clean after the face wash. Georgie sat up, looking like she'd been dunked in a slime machine, like the ones that they use in game shows on the telly!

Alex couldn't stop laughing, much to Georgie's disgust until he himself was chased by Psycho, the mad white rabbit with blood red eyes that freely roamed the village green in front of the post office on Honeypot Lane. Many people had tried to capture and tame the beast of Codswallop. All had failed!

"Help me, Georgie!" Alex screamed as he desperately ran around the green, the demented bunny gaining ground on him, his evil eyes glowing like two burning hot coals in the snow!

Georgie sat down on the grass, grinning. "I know; I'll sunbathe here for a while, get a tan and then pretend that I am a giant carrot! He's sure to chase me then!" She laughed, as Alex scrambled up the nearest tree whilst Psycho madly jumped up and down beneath him, its sharp claws scratching deeply into the trunk. It was only when the bunny ran out of puff and fell soundly asleep below him half an hour later that Alex felt safe and brave enough to climb down, slowly tip-toeing past the snoring rabbit before making a hasty escape.

"Thanks for nothing," Alex sulked, picking up the bike before the two of them began to trudge up a hill. Georgie put her arm around his slumped shoulders. "You've got to admit it was pretty funny, dude!" She smiled, her green eyes shining brightly.

"Only if you were at the bottom of the tree looking up!" Alex said, grinning despite himself.

Georgie delved into the bottom of the bag. "Anyway, look on the bright side! We've only got to deliver this last magazine and we're done! Tell you what, I'll buy you a massive ice cream and then we'll go off and do something fun for the rest of the day."

In her hands, she held a copy of Crackpot's Inventions Monthly. On the front, it had a picture of a large golden robot, wearing an apron, with the words 'Bumper September Issue!' printed in bold letters across the face of it. Alex's face brightened at the prospect of yet more free food.

"Excellent!" he said, with a newly found spring in his step. "So where have we got to deliver that to then?"

Georgie looked at the address written in pencil on the bottom of the magazine. "I can't quite make it out, it appears to be written in some secret code!" Alex sighed deeply, taking the magazine from Georgie. Turning the magazine upside down, he then passed it back to her. "Wow that was clever!" She chuckled, her cheeks reddening slightly as she read aloud the address. "Slipp Manor. That's right at the top of the hill, past the old mill, isn't it Alex? Alex?"

Alex's eyes were now as wide as saucers and he had gone as pale as a ghost, his knuckles white as he tightly grasped the handlebars of the bike. "S-S-Slipp Manor? We can't g-go there." He stuttered, nervously.

"Why ever not?" Georgie asked, as her cousin leant the bike against a nearby wall and shakily sat down on the kerb by the side of the road.

Alex gulped, shaking his head repeatedly. "My parents have told me never to go anywhere near Slipp Manor. They say that some crazy dude lives there. No one's seen him properly for years! He orders all his shopping and stuff online and gets it delivered. My mate's dad is a milkman and he used to leave sixteen pints of milk, in a crate, on the doorstep there every day. That was until the morning he saw a long, grey mechanical claw stretch out from the front door and snatch the crate in as he was driving away. Now he leaves it by the gate at the bottom of the drive and drives away as quickly as he can. Well, as quickly as you can in a milk float, that is. No one ever chooses to go to Slipp Manor, not unless they really have to."

"What a load of rubbish!" Georgie snorted, striding up the hill. "I'm not scared of old wives' tales! And anyway, I won't get paid for my round unless I deliver everything in my bag!" Alex cycled frantically after her.

"Can't you just chuck the magazine in the bushes or something and say that you delivered it?" He pleaded with her as she marched along ahead of him.

Georgie stopped and turned to look at him suddenly. She tilted her head and crossed her arms. Alex knew and feared that look. Here it comes, he thought. The lecture.

"Oh yeah, right! And then if Slipp phones up Mr Jones at the Village Store and complains that he hasn't received this month's magazine and then Jonesy calls the police and says that there's a magazine thief in the village and they come around and question me and I burst into tears and blurt out 'IT WAS ME!!! Lock me up and throw away the key! I threw the magazine away because my scaredy-cat cousin didn't want to go to the house because of the nutter with the metal hand that lives there'. And then they'll put me in a prison for children, where I can't watch television, or use my EYE-TAPP to text my friends or use my apps, or surf the Internet, or eat sweets, or wear my Pantora bracelet or any brightly coloured designed clothes, just grey, torn rags. My poor Mum and Dad will shake their heads and say, 'We are so ashamed. We never thought that we'd end up with a jailbird for a daughter', and they'll be shunned by the whole village, with people pointing at them, shouting, 'Look! It's the magazine thief's parents!' So, they'll have to walk around wearing hats and dark glasses so that no one recognises them, or they'll be forced to move away and live in a caravan, next to a donkey rescue farm and..."

"Okay, Okay, you win!" As usual, Alex gave in, partly because he didn't want anyone to think he was a wimp, but mainly because if he didn't stop Georgie talking, she was likely to run out of breath and faint, as she'd once done before! Nobody was better at making a drama out of something than his cousin! She'd had years of practice!

"I'll come to Slipp Manor with you because I don't think that you should go up there all on your own. But if I see or hear anything even slightly unusual, I'll be out of there faster than Psycho the killer bunny!"

A huge smile beamed across Georgie's freckled face as she hugged her cousin tightly, planting a large, wet kiss on his cheek. "Gerroff you big softie, one of my friends might see me!" Alex growled, wiping his face with his sleeve as he tried to escape her clutches.

With that, the two of them turned and made their way up the hill toward the

tall, run-down building that stood alone at the very top of it. Far away from its

nearest neighbour. Far away from the rest of the village that lay behind them.

Chapter 2 – The House on the Hill.

By the time they'd reached the large, cast iron gates that stood guarding the driveway of Slipp Manor, a huge black thundercloud loomed above them, casting a heavy shadow over the old house and its overgrown garden. Alex and Georgie glanced at one another and then looked back down the hill to the rest of Codswallop, which was still covered by brilliant sunlight.

"That's it I'm off", said Alex, turning the bike around sharply to go.

"Don't be so silly," Georgie said as she placed her hand on one of the gates. It groaned, like an old man in pain, as she pushed it open. "Come on, the sooner we deliver this, the more time we'll have to chill later!" She started to walk up the long windy path, the gravel crunching loudly beneath her shoes. Alex rested the bike against the gatepost and began to scurry behind her, his eyes anxiously scanning the garden as he followed.

"Here goes nothing." He gulped, hurrying to catch up with his cousin.

As they approached the house, Alex noticed that almost all the windows had been boarded with old wooden planks. Large cobwebs hung from them, like lace curtains. All except one, where its shutter banged backwards and forward in the wind, that had now begun to pick up. Alex thought that could see lots of tiny eyes peering at him through the gaps in the wood, but he shook his head. "Nah, you're just imagining things." He muttered, more to himself than anyone else, as he rubbed his eyes vigorously.

"Come on slowcoach!" Georgie shouted back as she stepped up onto the porch in front of the house. A long, frayed brown cord dangled in front of the door, a knot at the bottom of it where a handle should be. "Looks like the thing that they used to pull to flush an old Victorian toilet with!" She laughed, pulling it down firmly. A loud bell echoed in an empty hallway, hidden from view by the door.

"What on earth are you doing?!" Screeched Alex shrilly.

Georgie turned and winked at him. "I want to see what all the fuss is about!" She smiled cheekily.

"Have you gone totally off your head?" Alex gasped, quickly hiding behind one of four old, stone pillars that held the porch up. He held his breath as he waited, ready to run at the first sign of danger, his heart pounding like a drum against the walls of his chest. There was no reply.

"See. After all that, it looks like he's not in anyway!" Georgie said, peering through the letterbox. Alex peeped around the pillar and then tiptoed slowly toward the door. He shoved Georgie over so that he could look too. The hall did indeed appear empty, except for a couple of scruffy looking cats that lay fast asleep on the steps of a large wooden staircase at the far end of it.

"Quick, just push the magazine through and let's get out of here!" Alex pleaded, stepping back away from the door. Georgie sighed, nodded, rolled the magazine up and started to poke it through the letterbox.

Suddenly, there was a loud whirring sound as a large steel claw shot out through the letterbox, past the magazine, catching Georgie tightly on the wrist, pulling her quickly toward the door.

"AAAAAAAAAAAARGH!" Georgie screamed in terror. "Something's got hold of my arm!" Alex rushed forward, wrapped his arms around her waist and began to pull her as hard as he could. But it was no good, Georgie's arm was wedged firmly in the letterbox. "It's no use, it's got me in its death grip! I'm doomed! Run, save yourself!" She said, dramatically.

"Not if I can help it, heave!" Alex cried, placing a foot on the doorframe as he strained to free her again. But as he pulled, his foot slipped, causing him to lose hold of Georgie, falling to the ground and landing with a thud. "Ouch! My ass!" He exclaimed, rubbing his bottom frantically. "I'm so sorry. Hold on, I'll go get us help from somewhere."

"Don't you leave me, Alexander Daniel McClellan!" Screamed Georgie, continuing, "Please! If we could only find a...wait! I think that I can hear footsteps!" They looked nervously at one another. Alex knelt by the door and looked through the letterbox again, past Georgie and the claw that remained tightly locked on her wrist.

Inside the house, he thought that he could make out a tall, thin figure standing at the top of the stairs. Alex leant back and rubbed his eyes again.

"What can you see?" Georgie pleaded. Alex shook his head.

"I'm not sure." He returned his eyes to the letterbox again. Yes, there was a figure, dressed all in white from head to toe, only now it was walking slowly down the staircase, a gloved hand running along the bannister as it went, as though moving in slow motion, from one stair to the next. It wore large boots on its feet, which thudded heavily on the wooden stairs. A helmet, with a black, mirrored visor, covered its head.

"What do you see? What is it? Who's coming?" Georgie asked desperately, her free hand tugging hard on Alex's T-shirt, trying to get his attention.

"I dunno, I'm really not sure," Alex whispered gravely, as he moved away from the door. He turned toward his cousin and held her by her shoulders. "I can't be sure…I can't see its face, but it looks like a sort of spaceman or it could be…" he swallowed hard, "a ghost!"

Georgie quickly bent down as far as she could and tried to look through the letterbox for herself. The strange figure was now upon them.

"AAAAAAAAAAAAAAAAARGH!" They both screamed as the door suddenly swung open, pulling them both in with it. Alex landed in a crumpled heap beside the feet of the figure, Georgie still hung from the door. He looked up as the figure looked back down at him, unmoving, its head first tilting left, then right, as if trying to decide what to do.

Slowly, it raised an arm and extended it toward Alex. A raspy, metallic voice echoed from behind the visor. *"Lemi-el-poo-hup"*.

Alex's mouth fell wide open in astonishment as he continued to stare upwards, his frightened face mirrored in the helmet's visor.

"Lemi el poo hup". The figure repeated as Alex sat there, motionless.

Georgie shook her head and shouted from behind Alex. "WE. DON'T. SPEAK. YOUR. LANGUAGE. THIS. IS. CODSWALLOP!"

Slowly the figure turned and looked at Georgie, who was still hanging from the door. "WE. COME. IN. PEACE! DO. YOU. UNDERSTAND?"

The figure again began to move its head, first to one side and then the other as though it was trying to work out what Georgie was saying. It then nodded.

"AYE-SAYED", its voice boomed, as it slowly began to remove its helmet.

Alex covered his eyes in case the creature had laser beams that would melt them both. The figure slowly took off the helmet to reveal…. a shiny bald head, a pair of round milk bottle glasses and a wispy ginger beard!! Georgie was relieved to see the kindly face of a man beneath the helmet.

"I said, let me help you up!" The man said cheerfully as he turned back around and smiled warmly at Alex.

"Oh, brother!" Alex sighed in relief as he was pulled to his feet.

"So sorry to frighten you, young man. Please allow me to introduce myself. My name's Slipp, Lord Thyme-Slipp. Here. Take my card." The man said, producing a crumpled and battered business card from the pocket of his white suit. Alex took the card cautiously and peered closely at it.

"Cool. I'm Alex and that's my cousin Georgina." He said, pointing distractedly across the hall. "So, what's with the space suit?" Alex asked gesturing towards him, passing back the card. Slipp looked at him strangely, a puzzled look on his lined face.

"What?" He looked down at his outfit. "Oh, these old things. No, no it's not a space suit, they're my overalls! I'm using an automatic painting machine I've invented to do the ceiling in my bedroom and I didn't want to splatter myself with paint! You see, it's just a little bit, erm, unpredictable!"

"Automatic painting machine? That sounds wicked! I love gadgets and that sort of stuff! Can I see it? Please?" Alex asked excitedly, eagerly jumping up and down on the spot.

Slipp seemed slightly taken aback. "Would you? Really?" He replied, excitedly adding, "Yes, yes, of course! This way my dear boy".

The two of them began to hurry toward the staircase, eagerly chatting away to one another.

"HELLLLLLLOOOOOOOOOOOOOOOOOOO THERE! Haven't you both forgotten something?" Georgie shouted after them angrily, pointing at her trapped arm.

Alex and Slipp stopped and turned. "What? Oh, silly me! I'm so sorry, Hang on for just a minute, my dear girl. We'll have you out of there in a moment!" Slipp responded, blushing slightly as he walked toward the door, Alex sheepishly followed closely behind, embarrassed that he'd forgotten his cousin! He waved nervously at Georgie, who sniffed loudly and turned her head away. Slipp patted Georgie gently on the head before carefully peering behind the door. "Ah yes, I can see what the problem is."

"Yes, I've been attacked and I'm flipping stuck in the letterbox!" Georgie replied, angrily.

"No, no, not at all." Slipp laughed from behind the door before continuing, "The door-opener-letter-grabber has just jammed, that's all. If I just unscrew this bit here and twist there…." Georgie could hear a scraping and banging of metal as Slipp worked on the other side of the letterbox, muttering under his breath as he did so. "Now, when I count to three, try and pull your arm out. One, two, thr…." But before he had finished counting, Georgie had freed her arm and gone flying across the hallway, landing in a crumpled heap on the floor opposite her cousin.

Slipp poked his head back from around the door and clapped his hands together loudly. "Excellent, most excellent!"

"I'm glad that you think so! "Georgie moaned as she got up, rubbing her bottom carefully.

"You've got a dusty butt now!" Alex started to snigger before thinking better of it. Slipp walked toward them, carrying the now lifeless mechanical claw in his hands.

"I am really sorry about that. I used to use it to fetch the milk in, but, for some reason, they don't deliver here anymore." Alex and Georgie looked at each other knowingly but said nothing. "Rather than junk it off, I adapted it to open the door or collect the post for me instead," Slipp added.

"Well, it looks like it's also good at catching children's arms too!" Georgie replied crossly. "Well, thank you for freeing me, Lord Thyme-Slipp, we'd best be going home now."

Slipp looked a little disappointed. "Oh, must you, so soon? You're welcome to stay for a bit. I don't get that many visitors and I miss having guests. Won't you two stop for just a little while? After all, it looks like it might begin to rain soon." Slipp peered through the doorway as though to confirm this.

The children looked at each other nervously.

"You see," Alex began, "our parents say that we shouldn't really talk to strangers and, well, let's face it, you are very, very strange! The whole village thinks so!"

Slipp looked both stunned and surprised by the statement. "Really? Do they? Well, I never! No, no, your parents are quite right. You shouldn't speak to strangers. And you must make sure that you keep yourself safe from harm. Well, I suppose that this is it then. Goodbye." He nodded as he opened the door fully for them.

Alex and Georgie walked carefully towards it as Slipp continued speaking quietly to himself. "Not that I'm a stranger to Codswallop. After all, I've lived here all my life. Everyone in the village knows of the Thyme-Slipp family, but I totally understand. Can't be too careful nowadays."

The children stopped and turned in the doorway to look back at Slipp as he sighed and trudged sadly away from the door. He continued to speak softly, more to himself than anyone else.

"I admit that I keep myself to myself, but that's only because I'm incredibly shy and don't feel comfortable around loads of people." Slipp sat down slowly on the bottom stair, resting his chin in his hands.

Alex knew he shouldn't but he couldn't help himself from asking. "Why is it easier not being around people?" Georgie dug an elbow into his ribs as though telling him to shut up, but he continued speaking anyway. "Don't you ever go out then?"

Slipp sighed sadly. "No, not much. It all goes back to when I was about your age. I was teased and bullied quite a bit when I was a younger. Short, chubby, glasses and ginger hair, a good combination when you're at school! I was an easy target for the bullies, especially on the playground. So, to avoid them, I'd take myself off to a quiet corner somewhere, notebook in hand. I've been fortunate in that I have a vivid imagination so I can drift easily into my own little world. I'd also have these weird and wonderful ideas for gadgets and inventions which I'd scribble down too. The few friends I had just wanted to play football or kiss-chase or '*IT*' or swap cards with one another. But as I was more interested in sciences, nature and world around me, I'd spend all my time coming up with ideas, drawing designs. Then, as I got a little older, I began to invent, create and build things. Not because I wanted to become rich and famous. Quite the opposite in fact as my family were pretty well off. No, all I ever wanted to do was help people and try to make life easier and better for them."

Alex and Georgie couldn't help but begin to feel sorry for the forlorn looking figure who now sat before them.

Slipp sighed deeply before continuing, as though reliving the events of his past. "Problem was, the more I stayed at home working on my designs, the more wrapped up I became in my projects. My friends, the few that I had, used to knock for me to go out and play, but I'd always say that I was too busy and couldn't come out. It wasn't long before they stopped calling for me. Eventually, I lost touch with them all. Most of them have moved away, and the ones who still live in the village I don't see, them having families, friends and lives of their own. Sadly, both my parents died within months each other when I was a teenager, leaving me this house and the Slipp family fortune. I have no other close family, except a few distant relatives scattered here and there who I wouldn't know if I passed them in the street. All I have now to keep me company are my journals, designs and inventions. I know I may appear a little odd and eccentric, but I promise you that I'd never cause any harm to anyone."

By now, Alex and Georgie had moved away from the door and had sat down beside Slipp on the stairs.

"So, you live in this big old house all on your own then?" Georgie asked.

Slipp nodded. "Yes, just me. Well, apart from the Kitty Clan of course!"

"The what?" asked Alex, curiously.

"The Kitty Clan!" Slipp repeated, more excitedly this time. Seeing the confused look on the children's faces, he smiled broadly. "Ah, probably best that I show you then," he laughed and stood, his knees cracking and popping with the effort, causing the children to wince. Slipp cupped his hands on either side of his mouth and loudly called out. "Munch-munch-munch-Muncheeeeeeeeeeeeeeeeees!"

At first, there was silence, then, slowly, came the sound of lots of tiny feet, pitter-pattering from all around them.

Suddenly it appeared that everywhere the children looked there was a cat! Big cats, small cats, old cats, young cats, fat cats, thin cats. Black ones, white ones, gingers ones, fluffy ones, multi-coloured ones. Some missing ears, some missing tails. There was even one missing a leg! Cats of all different breeds, shapes and sizes. But there was one thing that they all obviously shared. They all loved the sound of their owner's voice!

In just a few minutes, there was a sea of fur sitting patiently in front of them at the foot of the stairs, purring away, happily. Alex tried to count them, but it proved to be difficult to do so accurately as they all seemed to merge into one another. He was pretty sure that there were at least seventy moggies gathered before them, expectantly waiting for their master's next command.

"What are they all waiting for?" Alex whispered to Georgie as the cats looked eagerly at Slipp, never taking their eyes off him.

"Dunno," Georgie replied with a shrug of her shoulders.

"Now, just watch this," Slipp said quietly, winking. "Gizmooooooooooo!" Suddenly, almost immediately, the buzzing sound of an engine echoed around them. Sat on what appeared to be a remote-controlled car, was a large, grey and white cat, its eyes as wide as saucers. The cat's paws appeared to be locked onto a small steering wheel as it moved the wheel frantically, first one way and then the other, back and forth, causing the wheels of the car to screech as it slid across the wooden floor.

"The rest of the cats won't go into the kitchen until Gizmo goes in first. He's the Kitty King!" Slipp chuckled as Gizmo whizzed across the hall and sped toward the kitchen.

"Why's he in a car?" asked Georgie.

"Because he's old, fat and very lazy!" came the reply.

"Who's controlling it?" added Alex.

"He is!" Slipp laughed as Gizmo sped toward the kitchen doorway. "Took him ages to learn how to steer…"

But before he could complete the sentence, the cat let out a load "MEOWWWWWWWWWWWWWWWW!" as it turned a corner, before crashing headfirst into a heavy wooden door!

 "Oops! I forgot to open the kitchen door! Bet that hurt!" Slipp quickly jumped up and made his way across the hallway, with the children in close attendance. They found the cat lying flat on his back, eyes staring at the ceiling, the car upside down next to him, engine whirring, wheels still spinning rapidly. Slipp carefully picked Gizmo up and started to stroke him gently. The cat, slightly dazed, looked back at him, its eyes rolling in all directions as a large bump began to form on the top his head. However, once Slipp started to stroke him, he began to purr loudly, sounding more like a pigeon cooing!

"I'm so sorry, old boy. Totally my fault. Now, let me see our young friends off, then we can have biscuits and some nice, warm milk."

"Biscuits? Did you say biscuits?" Alex's ears pricked up like a mini radar at the very mention of the word.

Georgie shook her head. "He meant cat biscuits, you numpty!"

Slipp smiled and nodded.   "Yes, I did, though I shall probably have a couple of nice chocolate digestives with cocoa myself". Georgie and Alex looked at each other and grinned naughtily.

"Well I suppose we could stay for a few more minutes, just to keep you company of course," Georgie said, continuing, "but we must go be going soon after that."

A huge smile cracked across Slipp's face as he nodded in agreement. "But of course! Excellent, excellent! I'll go put the milk on."

And with that, he flung open the door and hurried into the kitchen, followed by a succession of furry feet pounding the floor, which just about managed to drown out the sound of the two children's rumbling tummies!

Chapter 3 – The Time Skipper.

Alex and Georgie looked around in wonder as they entered the kitchen. Everywhere they turned they saw strange looking devices and weird contraptions scattered around the place. There was even a small model railway track which went around the entire perimeter of room!

"Please sit down, sit down!" Slipp said, clapping his hands sharply together. Two stools, with wheels on each of their legs, shot out from under the table that stood in the centre of the kitchen. They scooped the children up in their bucket seats and took them back to sit at the table-top.

"Wicked!" Alex exclaimed as Slipp fetched a glass milk jug from the fridge and poured all its contents into a saucepan that sat on an old coal fired stove.

"I'll just put this on to boil, and feed my lovelies," Slipp said adding, "then we can have a biscuit or two and a chat!"

Slipp took a poker from beside the stove and, opening a small door on it, stoked the coals that now burned even brighter inside. Putting the poker back in the coal scuttle, he then stamped firmly on a large red button that stuck out of the tiled floor.

At the far end of the kitchen, another shiny mechanical hand, like the one that had caught Georgie, but smaller, shot out, holding a packet of cat biscuits between its claws. Slowly it tilted and tipped its contents into a large, purple funnel that hung above a train that sat on the track. The Kitty Clan were all sat patiently in a circle around the edge of it, like passengers waiting at a station. Once the funnel was totally full, a small door opened at its bottom, dropping some cat biscuits into the first of the numerous trucks that were coupled to the engine at the front, stretching all along the track.

When the first truck was full, the funnel closed and the engine began to inch along the track until the next truck was positioned beneath the funnel and was filled again. Each time a truck was filled, the funnel would close and the train would move along again, slowly repeating the process. Alex and Georgie looked on in amazement as one by one the trucks filled up and moved along the entire length of the track.

Finally, when the last container was full, the mechanical hand put the cat biscuits away and flicked a switch on the wall beside the cupboard. A piercing whistle blew, causing the children to cover their ears briefly as all the cats moved forwards and began to eat from the trucks that were lined up neatly and perfectly in front of them. The sound of crunching and purring filled the room. Alex and Georgie grinned at one another at the sight they were witnessing before them.

 "That's brilliant!" Alex cried out as Slipp began to pour the hot milk that had boiled in the meantime into three large mugs.

"Thank you," Slipp smiled, "one of my older, but more successful inventions." He handed each of them a mug before sitting at the table opposite them.

"Biscuit, er, I am terribly sorry I didn't quite catch your names?"

"Alex. Georgie. Yes, we'd love a biscuit." Alex said enthusiastically, pointing to himself and his cousin.

"Pleased to meet you. Again!" smiled Slipp as he flicked another switch that was to the side of the table. From its centre, a long clear plastic tube shot out in front of them, causing the children to jump. Beneath the table came a whooshing noise that sounded like a vacuum cleaner.

"The rule is, whatever you catch, you eat!" Slipp laughed loudly as digestives, jammy dodgers, bourbon biscuits and chocolate chip cookies began to fly out of the tube, shooting high up into the air. Alex and Georgie dived around like a couple of mad goalkeepers, catching and grabbing as many biscuits as they could. Georgie dropped quite a few, which were quickly whisked away by the cats sat nearest to her on the floor. Predictably though, Alex was like an octopus, scooping biscuits up in his out-stretched shirt, when he could gather no more in his hands. When they both had more biscuits than they could carry, Slipp flicked the switch off again. They sat at the table, munching away happily on their haul.

"So, do you sell many of your inventions, Lord Slipp?" Georgie mumbled in between bites.

Slipp shook his head, crumbs flying from his whiskers. "Unfortunately, not! There's been the odd one or two but generally, so far, no. But I'm ever hopeful. No matter, I have these wonderful things all to myself!" He winked at them both, a smile dancing on his chocolate smeared lips.

"Then how do you pay for all this, especially with all the cats that you have. It must cost you a fortune to feed and look after them." Alex asked, stuffing another jammy dodger, his twelfth, into his biscuit-filled mouth.

"As I said, the family fortune. My family were very rich, so I've never needed to worry about money. I've got more than enough to get by on. No, the problem with selling my inventions, as I see it, is that people want something that's totally life-changing, not only to improve it," he took a large gulp of his cocoa, "Everything nowadays is so easy. TV dinners, internet shopping, fast food, home deliveries, those sorts of things, nobody really needs or want what

I invent. Well, at least, not until now." Slipp had a glint in his eye as he looked over the rim of his mug at the children sitting before him.

"Oh, it's no good!" he said hesitantly, peering over his glasses, leaning closer toward them across the table. "I'm so excited! I've got to tell someone!"

"Tell us what? Georgie asked curiously. Alex carried on munching on another biscuit, like a hungry hamster!

Slipp rubbed his chin, as though he was carefully weighing up his options. "I know that I've only just met you, but you genuinely seem like nice children and as there's no one else I can share this with…"

"What? WHAT?!" Georgie demanded.

"Have you ever done something and then wished you hadn't? Or lost something that was special to you and tried to remember where you were when you last had it?"

The children thought long and hard for a moment. "I know!" Alex piped up, "A couple of years ago, when I was playing 'Stuck in the Mud' one playtime, I accidentally ripped my trousers doing the splits as I tried to escape my mate. Everyone could see my pants! They all started to laugh and point and take the mickey out of me. I was so embarrassed"

"I'm not surprised, "Georgie sniggered, "I've seen the state of your pants on the washing line!"

"Shut up Georgie!" If you're going to make fun of me…"

"No, please carry on Alex," interrupted Slipp, "I really want to hear your story. Go on."

Alex stuck out a biscuity-coated tongue at his cousin.

"Ewww! You're so gross!" Georgie sneered back at him.

"Anyway," Alex continued, "I had to wear this tatty pair of baggy pink jogging bottoms out of the spare PE kit box for the rest of the day as there were no spare school trousers and Mum and Dad were at work. What was even worse was I had to go home in them! I remember wishing that it was all just a bad dream and that I'd wake up and everything would be all right. But it wasn't. And I didn't," Alex shook his head sadly, "And now, even though I've moved up into year 5, I still get teased or reminded about it. I so wish that it had never happened at all!"

Slipp jumped up, pointing enthusiastically at Alex. "Exactly! That's my point! Every single day, we make mistakes. Some little, some not so. And generally, we can't do anything about it or it's too late to. But what if you could travel back in time for just a few minutes, or a matter of hours to change what you'd done. Or to put everything right? Would you welcome the chance to?"

Georgie and Alex looked at each other slightly confused.

"Well yeah, of course, but that's totally imposs-" Georgie began, but before she could finish her sentence, Slipp was already up out of his chair and heading quickly towards the kitchen door.

"Follow me! To the living room!" he cried out as he sped across the hall, leaving the two children staring at one another, open-mouthed.

"I told you he was a nutter," whispered Alex, "but I've got to see what he's on about." Georgie nodded as the two of them jumped down from their chairs and quickly raced out after him, Alex grabbing another couple of biscuits as he went.

When they reached the living room, they found Slipp sitting in the centre of a scruffy blue sofa opposite an old colour television, which was blaring away noisily, a succession of images filling its flat screen. Between the sofa and the TV, stood on an oriental rug, was a small black wooden coffee table, with a remote control resting in the middle of it. Two long cables ran from the back of the television, under the rug and were attached to the wooden feet of the sofa by two big metal bulldog clips.

"Behold! I present to you my greatest invention, The Time Skipper!" Slipp announced proudly, extending his arms out wide.

Georgie and Alex looked around the room. "Erm, ok. Where is it then?" Alex enquired, scratching his head. Slipp patted the sofa on either side of him with both hands.

"Come, join me and I'll show you." The children shrugged their shoulders and sat down on either side of him, as though to humour him. "Are you sitting comfortably?" he asked. Slowly, they both nodded back. "Good, let's begin". Slipp leant forward and starting to tap the keys on the brightly coloured remote control.

"What are you doing exactly?" Georgie asked as Slipp continued to frantically type away."

"Erm, what? Oh, yes, sorry. This is just like one of those all-in-one remote controls that you can get in any old pound shop. Only it has a few extra little functions that I've added. Now it's the key to making the Time Skipper work successfully. Look." he said, holding the remote up to them. He pointed his index finger at its large digital display. "See this? It says that the time is currently 11:30 on Saturday 2nd of September. Is that correct?"

Alex looked suspiciously at his watch. "Uh-huh, give or take a few seconds."

"Excellent, excellent. Now, I am going to change the time back to 10:45. Now, look what happens after I point it at the black box under the television."

35

Slipp pointed the control towards the TV. Alex and Georgie peered at the bright red numbers that were now flashing on what looked like an old DVD player that sat on the stand under the television. "Do you see?"

"Wow, fancy that! It says 10:45 too!" Georgina added sarcastically. Alex nudged her, but Slipp was far too engrossed in what he was doing to notice.

"Good, good. Now could you both put these on," he said, passing them each a pair of dark glasses. They looked like the type of glasses that you'd wear to watch a 3D movie, except the sides were also covered in, almost turning them into goggles. Alex and Georgie immediately did as they were asked.

"I think my pair are broken. I can't see anything at all through these!" Alex protested loudly.

"Don't worry Alex, you're not supposed to!" Slipp laughed as he put his own pair of dark glasses on, taking his normal glasses off in doing so. "Now, please sit back deeper into the sofa, as we may be in for a slightly bumpy ride." The three of them leant back as Slipp pressed the large "ENTER" button right in the middle of the remote control.

First, there was silence, but soon a loud whirring sound came from the black box as the numbers on its display flashed once, then twice, before changing from red to amber and, finally, to green. After a few moments, the lights stopped flashing and a high-pitched beeping sound, like the noise a microwave oven makes after it's finished cooking, came from the box.

"Ok, we're here!" announced Slipp, jumping up from the sofa, crashing into the coffee table, before falling to the floor. "Whoops, forgot to take my specs off! "he said, sheepishly, pulling off his dark glasses, putting his other ones back on. "Hurry, we haven't got that much time!" And with that, he scuttled out of through the living room door back into the hall.

Alex and Georgie slowly removed their glasses, and looked at each other, feeling slightly confused.

"But we haven't gone anywhere!" Alex whispered into his cousin's ear.

"Don't you think I've noticed that you numpty!" she replied, adding, "I think that you may be right about him being a nut-" Just then, Slipp called loudly from the hallway.

"Are you two coming? Quick, it's nearly time." The children sighed, shrugged their shoulders and trudged out into the hall to see Slipp opening the kitchen door wide.

"Now, please sit down at the foot of the stairs." he said, turning and walking back toward them.

"What for?" Georgie asked.

"Why, to watch me set things right!" At the top of his voice, Slipp called out loudly. "Munch-munch-munch-Muncheeeeeeeeeeeeeeeeeees!"

"Haven't we been here before? They'll still be full from earl-" Alex began to ask, only to be interrupted again by the now familiar sound of tiny feet pitter-pattering around the house. Everywhere they looked, the cats reappeared, carpeting the floor in front of them.

"Have to admit, this is a bit freaky," answered Georgie as all the Kitty Clan seemed to gather in the same places, as before. Just a few minutes later, there they all were again sitting patiently before Slipp at the foot of the stairs.

"So, are they going to wait for Gizmo again?" Alex whispered, turning toward Slipp. Slipp smiled back at him.

"Again? No, not at all. This is the first time they've waited for her today. Just watch. Gizmooooooooooooooooo!" Slipp bellowed. Once again, the sound of wheels screeching across the floor came from a room to the left of the hall.

And, as before, there was Gizmo, mounted on the remote-control car, frantically moving the steering wheel, first one way, then the other, as he sped again towards the kitchen.

"You see, I wanted to show you how the Time Skipper can change things," Slipp said as Gizmo headed toward the kitchen doorway. He let out a load "MEOWWWWWWWWWWWWWWWW!" and sailed through the door into the kitchen, rapidly followed by all the other cats, leaving Slipp and the children alone in the now empty hallway.

"See, this time, to prevent him crashing into the kitchen door, I remembered to open it for him!" said Slipp, triumphantly, before the sound of banging and crashing from the kitchen drowned his voice out. Slipp winced.

"Unfortunately, it appears Gizmo forgot to use the brakes! Never mind, but can you see? By travelling back a little under an hour ago, I could change one tiny thing to stop him from getting that nasty bump on his head!"

Georgie smiled nervously. "Ok. Well. Yes. Great! Oh, is that the time? We'd best be getting along now, hadn't we Alex?" She elbowed her cousin in the ribs.

"Ow! Oh yes, that's right." Alex responded. "Thanks for the cocoa and biscuits, they were delicious," Alex said as Georgie grabbed his arm and hurried them toward the front door.

"Oh, of course. Lovely to meet you. Please do come again. Soon." Slipp said, disappointedly. "But, remember not a word about the Time Skipper to anyone. At least, not until I've patented it. Don't want anyone stealing my idea. After all, it's a real game changer!"

"Oh, trust me, Lord Slipp," Georgie called back before adding, "we won't be saying a word about this morning to anyone! Goodbye."

And with that, the children opened the door, waved before quickly scurrying down the path as fast as their legs could carry them, collecting Georgie's bike on the way. When they reached the gates at end of the drive, Georgie turned to Alex.

"Phew, I was worried that he might follow us! He seems to be a nice bloke but you're right. He's absolutely bonkers! Travelling back in time indeed! What nonsense! Anyway, we might just have enough time before lunch for that ice cream I promised you." said Georgie. Alex nodded as he carefully looked at his watch

"Too true. Yeah, plenty, it's only 11 o'clock and……huh?" Alex blinked and looked at his watch again, only much closer this time. "But that can't be right?" The two of them turned and then looked back at the old house.

"Nah, that's not possible," Georgie said as they hurried down the hill, back toward Codswallop and, hopefully, normality.

Chapter 4 – Lazing On-A-Not-So Sunny Afternoon.

The two of them had hardly said a word to one another by the time that they'd reached the brightly coloured van on the village green. Even then, it was just to say what they were going to get from the ice-cream man. It was only when they'd sat down on a bench nearby that they began to speak about the strange events they'd witnessed that morning.

"So, what do you reckon? That was all a bit weird, right?" Alex said finally, biting the bottom of his cone and sucking the ice-cream through it, making a noise sounding like that of a sink full of water emptying.

Georgie licked her lolly slowly. "Yep, just a bit! I've been thinking how he must have done it though. I reckon that when he was at the door, he only made it look like that he was opening it. It was probably still open after we left the kitchen. That means that all the cats had the chance to go back to where they were in the house when we followed Slipp into the living room."

She bit the top off the lolly then continued, her voice slightly muffled by the cold ice that filled her mouth. "That way, when we went back in the hall and he called them again, it looked like we'd gone back in time."

Alex thought briefly before responding. "But what about Gizmo and the car though?"

Georgie paused, pondering a reply. "She probably has loads of them all around the house."

Alex's slurping stopped as he sucked out the last of the ice-cream, before beginning to crunch on the cone.   "But why say that we had travelled back in time if we didn't? What would he do that for?"

"Don't you see, dummy?   He was pranking us!" laughed Georgie. "And you really fell for it, didn't you? Hook, line and sinker!"

"No, I didn't!" Alex protested. "Well, maybe, just a little bit. Just like you did!"

Georgie sighed and smiled at him, her lips pressed together, hiding her teeth. Not a sweet smile. No, the one that she used whenever she patronised him. "Oh Alex, really. I never fell for any of it. I only played along so that you didn't feel quite so foolish yourself," she shook her head knowingly before continuing, "Mind you, it was a pretty impressive trick, nearly fooled me. But not quite! Come on, don't feel bad, let's head back to my house. It'll be lunchtime soon and my Dad will be back from golf.   We can do something fun this afternoon if you'd like." Georgie jumped up from the bench and started to wheel the bike away.

Alex nodded and, stuffing what was left of the ice-cream cone into his mouth, got up to follow. "Lunch would be great. All that excitement has made me really hungry!"

They'd only walked on a little way before Alex stopped dead in his tracks.

"Hang on a second, if it was just a trick to fool us, then why does my watch show a different time to what it ought to be, clever-clogs?"

Georgie stroked her chin as she thought for a moment, then sighed again. "Well, it's pretty obvious really."

"It is?" Alex frowned, looking even more confused than ever.

Georgie nodded wisely. "Of course it is. He made sure that we sat either side of him on the sofa, didn't he? Me on the left, you on his right."

"Yes, so…?" Alex replied. Now his brain was really hurting, and it wasn't brain freeze caused by the ice-cream either!

"Seriously? Do I have to explain everything to you?" Georgie chuckled, "You wear your watch on your left arm, and that was next to him, right? So, he could easily have changed the time on it without you noticing!" Georgie looked smug as she continued, "That's why he made us wear those dark glasses so that we couldn't see him do anything!"

Alex's head throbbed even more." But I would have felt him do it?" he argued.

"Not if Slipp is really good at sleight of hand, you know, like the magicians on the telly.   Perhaps he's learnt how to do it from a book of magic, or with one of those conjuring set, like the one we gave Grandpa last Christmas." Georgie replied.

"But Grandpa was rubbish at it! I'll never forget the look on Dad's face when he borrowed his watch, wrapped it in a hankie and smashed it to pieces with a hammer!" Alex laughed. "To make matters worse, he blamed Dad for having the wrong type of watch when couldn't put it back together again and told him off for spoiling the trick on purpose!"

"Typical Grandpa," smiled Georgie, "but obviously Slipp is a lot better at magic tricks than him, don't you see?"

Alex shrugged his shoulders as they continued walking, checking the winder on his watch carefully. The two children were nearly back at Georgie's house before he spoke again. "I'm still not convinced, you know." he muttered as the two of them opened the back gate and walked into the garden, propping the bike up against an ivy-covered wall.

"Hi, Mum we're home!" Georgie shouted as they entered her house through the back door to her kitchen. Aunt Flora was up to her elbows in soapsuds in the sink.

"Hello, my little monsters. Well, there's a surprise! Back in time to be fed, I see!" Alex and Georgie gave each other a funny look as Flora continued. "I'm almost done washing Poxy. You did say that it was Dog Scrubbing Day today, didn't you?" Alex grinned a little guiltily as the family's Yorkshire terrier poked her head up between Flora's tattooed arms, looking more like a drowned rat than a dog! Poxy hiccupped, a load of soap bubbles floated out of her mouth up into the air like balloons let loose at a funfair.

Georgie grabbed a couple of canned drinks from the fridge and passed one to her cousin. "Where's Dad?" she asked, taking a swig from her can. Her mum nodded over her shoulder up towards the ceiling behind her.

"He's up in the office, busy working on that computer of his. Been up there ever since he got back from golf this morning." Georgie and Alex headed toward the stairs as Flora called after them. "Let your dad know that I'll be doing lunch soon, will you pet?"

"Ok Mum," Georgie replied as they made their way up the stairs in the direction of the spare bedroom that doubled as her father's home office. When they reached the doorway, Georgie dashed ahead of her cousin into the room where her father was working.

"Hi, Dad," she said happily, throwing her arms around her father's neck, kissing him gently on the cheek.

"Hello sweetheart," her Dad replied, turning away from the desk on his swivel chair to give her a massive hug, "and, surprise, surprise, there's Alex too!" He grinned, ruffling his nephew's hair. "I'm sure that you two are joined at the hip! How you doing little man?"

"Cool thanks, Uncle Jon." beamed Alex broadly. "What game you playing?"

Uncle Jon laughed, a huge grin filling his smooth, thin face. "I wish! No, I've got a new job that I've been asked to price up and quote by Monday morning. If the customer likes our price, it'll mean that I'll have enough work to keep the factory working full time over the winter. But, typically, it didn't arrive until late yesterday afternoon. I started to work on it at the factory but we had yet another power cut and I lost all the information that I'd entered, as well as some other files that I needed. So, rather than wait for the power to come back on or stay late last night, I decided to bring it home with me to work on over the weekend instead. That way, I can send it back to the customer first thing Monday, before anyone one else has a chance to quote for it!" he smiled, turning back to the screen.

"But if you lost all that stuff at work, how can you?" Georgie asked.

"Ah, fortunately, the computer at work is just a back-up. All the important information about the company is saved here on the home computer. I'd be totally stuffed if it wasn't saved on the hard drive here!" he said, patting the computer tower that stood next to the monitor on his desk.

"Will you be finished in time for lunch? Mum says that it's going to be ready soon." Georgie asked.

Her dad shook his head. "Probably not, I don't want to rush the quote and miss anything out. It's going to take me the best part of today, and some of tomorrow to finish it."

"Oh no, it won't!" boomed a voice from behind them. There, filling the doorway, stood the imposing figure of Aunt Flora, holding Poxy, who now resembled a fluffy stick of candy floss, tightly under her arm! "That's quite enough work for today, Jonathan. We're going out for the afternoon to see Angie and Kelly."

"But Flo, this is really important." Uncle Jon argued, pointing at his computer screen.

"And I'm not?" she cried.

"No, I didn't mean that, I meant that I've got to get this done for Monday…"

Flora shot him a fierce look. "You've worked late every night this week. You can have all the time you want tomorrow. Ok?"

Jon nodded reluctantly, as though accepting defeat. "All right dear, as you wish." Alex often wondered why Jon ever bothered arguing. Flora always got her way. He now realised where Georgie got her stubbornness from!

"Good. That's settled then. Lunch will be on the table in ten minutes." Flora announced, flouncing back downstairs, victorious, the matter now firmly closed.

Jon groaned. "Please kill me now! An afternoon spent with Flora's sister and her clown of a husband!" he angrily clicked the mouse to save his work and shut down the computer. "You don't fancy coming along as well do you kids? I could do with the support. I'll make it worth your while."

"No, we're good thanks, Dad," Georgie replied, "we're just going to chill here, listen to some music, watch TV, play games, stuff like that."

"Lucky you," Georgie's Dad grumbled as the three of them made their way down the stairs towards the large table that stood in the middle of their dining room. Alex's eyes almost exploded out of his head as he viewed what lay before him.

As per usual, Georgie's mum had put on a massive buffet for lunch. Laid out before them was a carnival of food. Ham, cheese, chicken pieces, salad, pickles, coleslaw, potato salad, crusty bread, sausage rolls and Alex's personal favourite – Homemade pork pie. Alex fairly dribbled his way around the table as he tried to decide what to put on his plate first. Much to his disappointment, the plate just wasn't big enough for him to fit everything on, but Alex was a master food stacker, honed by years of practice. If food gathering was an Olympic event, he'd be a gold medallist! By the time he had chosen what he wanted to eat, Alex had created an impressive food mountain, carefully balancing items on top of each other, based on their size and shape.

So expertly constructed was the tower of food, there was scarcely enough room to even squeeze a toothpick between any savoury gaps! Satisfied that he could fit no more on his plate, Alex sat down at the table, next to his uncle and began to tuck in. He had to admit that Aunt Flora had surpassed herself this time as everybody ate with great enthusiasm, speech replaced by the sound of munching and crunching of food, punctuated by an occasionally sigh or burp!

Finally, after Alex had demolished his fourth helping, the table looked like a deserted battlefield, with crumbs, stains, and food remnants strewn everywhere!

Alex and Georgie were left with the washing up as Georgie's parents went upstairs to get ready to go out, Jon still protesting, Flora still ignoring. Looking outside, through the kitchen window overlooking the sink, the children couldn't help but notice that the sky had turned grey and that small raindrops were beginning to splatter the window pane.

"Looks like we'll definitely have to stay indoors now," moaned Georgie. Alex nodded sadly, drying a plate with a flowery tea towel.

After a short while, her parents came back into the kitchen, Flora wearing a summery dress that was a size or two too small for her, Jon tugging at his collared shirt, loosening his tie slightly. "Are you both sure that you don't want to come with us?" Georgie's Dad said pleadingly. "After all it is raining now, so you're gonna be stuck inside this afternoon anyway."

Georgie and Alex looked at one another. "No thank you, there's plenty we can do here, isn't there Alex?" Georgie turned to her cousin, hoping that he'd pick up on her eagerness to remain at home.

Fortunately, Alex did, nodding enthusiastically in return. He could only really recall his last proper meeting with Angie when he was about seven. She'd rushed toward him, like a rampant hippo, gripped his cheek firmly between her thumb and forefinger and, pinching it roughly, declared that she 'loved cute little boys' and that she could just 'eat them all up!' Judging by how fat she was, Alex truly believed her, probably in one sitting as well! Ever since then, he avoided seeing her whenever there was a large family get together, feigning sleep or sickness on more than one occasion.

Georgie's Dad sighed in defeat, "Ok. Behave yourselves and don't get up to any mischief. Any problems, call us. Mrs King is at home next door. As it's Saturday, she'll be watching the wrestling, as usual, so you can always call on her. Just remember, I've got loads of important paperwork in my office so it's totally off limits today."

"But, Dad!" Georgie begged, opening her eyes as wide as possible at her father, looking like a forlorn beagle. It was no use as he shook his head back at her.

"Sorry sweetheart, but I've no choice. I've had to leave it in rather a hurry now, haven't I?" he replied, tilting his head in the direction of the departing Flora, who was travelling down the hall like a flowery tornado!

"Jonathan. Are you coming?" she called, pulling Poxy reluctantly on her lead behind her.

"Of course, dear," he replied rolling his eyes at Georgie. "Bye, kids, hopefully we'll be back by about six if I've got anything to do with it. Will you still be here then Alex?"

"I expect so, depends on what time Mum gets back from town. She shops until she drops normally, but she's with her BFF as well, so the credit cards might be taking quite a battering today!" laughed Alex.

"Jonathan, we're waiting!" screeched Flora in a voice so high that dogs would cover their ears and cower.

"Coming! See you guys later." And with that Georgie's Dad scuttled out the front door, grabbing his keys from the sideboard as he left. Georgie and Alex looked out the front window and waved after them as they walked down their driveway, before disappearing down the lane, umbrella raised, protecting them from the rain, which fell much heavier now.

"Well, it looks like we've got to stay in then? What do you want to do?" Georgie asked as they both slumped on the sofa bed in her play room.

Alex thought for a moment before answering. "PLAY, PLAY, PLAY!"

So, for the next few hours, that's exactly what they; cards, table tennis, snakes and ladders, draughts, tiddlywinks, hide and seek. Whilst they played, music blared around the house as they ate sweets, crisps, and biscuits and drank fizzy drinks until they almost burst.

They argued, bickered, teased, sulked and laughed with each other until finally collapsing in a heap, having exhausted almost everything of interest in the house.

"Wanna watch some telly?" Georgie asked, popping another gummy bear in her mouth,

"You got satellite or cable yet?" asked Alex, hopefully, already knowing the answer as Georgie shook her head. "Flexiflicks?" Again a 'No'.

"It's ok. Anyway, it's usually just sports and repeats on a Saturday afternoon." Alex said, laying on his back, watching a spider make its way slowly across the ceiling.

"What time is it?" asked Georgie. Alex looked at his watch.

"It's still only half past four. It'll be ages before your Mum and Dad are home." Georgie's face brightened. "What about your parents. Will they be back yet?"

"Nah, they said that whoever got home first would phone here and let me know."

They sat in a bored silence for a few more minutes, Georgie picking at her fingernails, Alex following the spider as it made its way toward the lampshade, where a previously woven web hung.

"So, what apps have you now got on your EYE-TAPP phone then, Georgie? Alex asked, hopefully expecting that his cousin would pass the phone to him to see for himself. His parents said that he was too young to have a phone of his own, which annoyed Alex immensely.

"Oh, just the usual." she replied, absent-mindedly platting an escaped strand of hair from her fringe. "Claptrapp, Infogram, Sickipaedia, Twaddle, Placebook, stuff like that."

49

"Cool, Can I play some games on it or look at the apps then please?" Alex asked eagerly. Georgie shot Alex a look as if to say 'No chance matey' and shook her head.

"Oh, come on Georgie, you know that I'll be careful with it. Let me have a go, please?"

Georgie shook her head firmly again. "It took me ages to convince Mum and Dad that I get it. It's the 14.4i, the very latest version with an Infinium Solar Cell powered by the sun!"

"Exactly!" argued Alex, "It'll never run out of battery, so you can let me play with it then. Yeah?

"No!" repeated Georgie firmly. "I'm under strict instructions not to let anyone use it other than me."

Alex sighed heavily. "But I'm not just anyone, I'm family! Plus, I'll be really careful not to get any smudges on it."

"Don't smudge. Don't matter. Don't care! This is one touchscreen that you can't touch!" Georgie insisted, patting her back-pocket firmly.

"It's so not fair!" Alex said crossly, "It's got so much cool stuff on it that you wouldn't begin to appreciate and I'm bored!"

Undeterred, Georgie shook her head again once more, before smiling mischievously. "Tell you what. Why don't we go on the computer and surf the internet instead? There's this wicked retro game site where you can play loads of different old arcade games, like dwarf tossing, badger bashing and penguin bowling!"

Alex's face started to brighten, but then he frowned, remembering what Jon had said as he left. "But your dad said that we couldn't use his office today."

"Only because he hasn't tidied it up. How hard could that be? If we move his paperwork carefully and put it all to one side, he won't mind us using the home computer. He'll be really pleased we've tidied up for him and, after all," Georgie fluttered her eyelids at Alex, trying to look cute as she continued, "I am Daddy's special little sunbeam!"

"Yeah, right!" Alex replied suspiciously, adding "But if we get in trouble with Uncle Jon..."

"We won't. Promise! Race yer!" Georgie laughed, jumping quickly out of her chair and mounting the stairs two at a time towards her father's office, closely followed by her younger cousin.

Georgie was right, it only took them a few minutes to gather up her Dad's paperwork, which was spread all around the room, into a neat pile beside his desk. Georgie sat in the swivel chair, her feet barely touching the floor as Alex pulled up a stool next to her. She turned on the computer. The screen slowly flickered into life and then asked them for a password.

"P...R...1...N...C...3...5...5, princess! Just like me!" Georgie smiled as she typed in the password. She hit the ENTER button triumphantly. After a couple of moments, the screen changed, with a picture of a young, skinny woman wearing only a tiny blue bikini appearing on it.

"Does Aunt Flora know that Uncle Jon's got a photo of a hot babe as his background?" Alex said pointing excitedly at the display.

"That's my mum Alex!" Georgie sighed disgustingly.

Alex stared in disbelief at the image in front of him. For some reason, the phrase 'who ate all the pies' came into his head as his cousin clicked the cursor on the internet icon that was on the toolbar at the bottom of the screen.

The old modem next to the computer flashed wildly, the tiny lights on it changing from amber to green.

Finally, the GOGGLE homepage filled the screen. Georgie began to type in the website address she wanted into the search engine's address bar.

"w w w, dot, gruesome, dash, games, dot, co, dot, u k." she said aloud, pounding the keys into submission before hitting the ENTER button firmly. After a little while, music and flashing lights filled the screen as it faded out and then changed again. Little 3D cartoon gif figures whizzed around all over the place as the home page appeared, with tinny old fashioned arcade music playing through the computer's speakers.

"Wicked!" Alex said as Georgie clicked the cursor on a button that said 'Hamster Hunt'.

"This is one of my favourites!" Georgie said as they waited for the game to load. "You have to see how many hamsters you can whack in a minute with a slipper. Back in the old days, games were not as good graphically, but you could do stuff that you can't do nowadays because someone would complain about it now. Here, let me show you how to play." Georgie used the arrow keys with one hand and clicked the mouse frantically with the other as various hamsters whizzed backwards and forwards across a hamster cage displayed on the screen. Each time one was hit, it would scream 'Eeeeeeek', before exploding like a red mushy tomato!

As the game progressed, different hamsters appeared. Some in hamster balls, some in toy cars, some dressed up in costumes. But all ended up the same way once hit - hamster ragu!

"Can I have a go?" Alex asked excitedly after Georgie finished the game with 38 hamster hits.

"Sure, do you want to play this, or something else?" She asked as a cartoon broom swept bits of hamster off the screen into the recycle bin.

"Another game please" Alex replied as he studied the list of game buttons that scrolled down the side of the web page. "Explode-A-Toad, Splat-A-Rat, Slug-A-Slug, Kick-A-Pig, Squash-A-Squid…" Then he stopped and shouted, pointing at the computer. "That one! I want to play that game!"

"Bash-A-Bunny?" Georgie said, "I ain't played that one. Is it any good?"

"No idea! But I sure like the sound of it!" Alex replied, "I can pretend that each rabbit is Psycho, Codswallop's mad, white rabbit! That way I can bash the heck out of him without worrying that he'll get me if I miss him!"

Georgie shrugged her shoulders and clicked on the game. A small greyed out box popped up on the screen saying, *'Do you want to run or save this file?'*

"What's that mean?" Alex asked. Georgie shook her head.

"Dunno, probably checking that we really want to play this game as we haven't played it before. But, if we don't like it, there's no point in saving it so…" she said as she clicked on the button that said *'RUN'*.

A new tab opened, with the words *'Loading, please stand by'* displayed on it as a white bar started filling up at the bottom of the screen, starting at *0%*.

"See. It won't be long now," Georgie said proudly, sitting back in the chair as the bar continued to grow.

'3%. 7%. 12%. 20%…'

Suddenly the words *'You do not have enough memory to run this application. Do you wish to free some disk space?'* appeared on the screen in front of them.

"What do we do now?" Alex asked as Georgie frowned at the screen.

"Don't you know anything?" Georgie sighed as she bit her bottom lip, "We free up some space for the new game. I have probably saved too many internet cookies on the computer, that's all." The screen gave them three choices. 'Yes, No' and 'Delete All Files'.

"Well we don't want to have to go through all of this again when we play another game, do we?" Alex said.

Georgie nodded. "No, you're right," she replied, clicking on the 'Delete All Files' option. "There. That ought to do the trick!"

Lots of little pages flew across the screen and disappeared into a tiny dustbin. Another screen popped up with the words 'Delete System Settings?'

"Can't remember playing that game," Georgie said as she clicked on the 'Yes to All' button, adding, "Silly name for a game anyway!"

The computer continued to whirr away. Five minutes later, the pages were still flying madly across the screen.

"Wow, that's a lot of cookies!" Alex smiled, turning to look at Georgie before adding, "Even I know that they're not the ones you eat! We'll be able to play loads of new games soon."

Georgie smiled back smugly at him, pleased that she'd dazzled her cousin with her brilliance yet again. "Dad will be so impressed that I know how to…" But the sound of the computer speakers beeping loudly stopped her dead in her tracks. They both looked intently at the screen. It was now totally blank and empty. Georgie hit the ENTER button. Nothing. She hit it again. Still nothing. It was only after continuing to hit it furiously that a little white line, like a cursor, appeared, flashing repeatedly in the top left-hand corner of the screen. Georgie pressed the ENTER button hard again. The white line continued to blink at them, but nothing else appeared.

"Uh-Oh!" Alex said nervously, "Try turning it off and on again. That's what my dad does when his work laptop freezes. He just reboots it."

"O-okay," Georgie replied suspiciously, as she clicked the computer's ON-OFF button twice. The computer fell silent, then the sound of a motor whirred again as the screen flickered back into life. But this time, there was no password and no blue bikinied woman. Just a blank screen with a small flashing white line in the top corner, as though winking at them, taunting them.

"Oh boy, are we in for it now!" exclaimed Alex, clapping his hands tightly to his face.

Georgie, who was on the verge of crying, gasped, "My Dad is going to ground me forever! I've totally destroyed his computer!"

Alex clambered under the desk and began rummaging through the cables that were there, looking like tangled spaghetti. "There must be something else we can do to fix it."

"Like what? Fix it using computer superglue or something? You great big idiot!" Georgie said crossly, adding, "It's all your fault anyway, telling me to turn the computer off to reboot it."

Alex looked stunned. "My fault? You were the one who said that we could go play on the internet this afternoon after your dad told us not to go in his office! And it was you who was Miss Know-it-all, deleting stuff when she really didn't know what on Earth she was doing!"

"I know!" Georgie wailed as she slumped to the floor and this time, the tears did flow as she began to cry. Despite feeling scared and angry himself, Alex couldn't stand to see his cousin so upset. He sighed and sat down next to her, putting an arm around her. Georgie leant in closely to him.

"Please don't cry. Don't cry, it'll be all right, you'll see." he said, patting her gently on the back.

Georgie's sobbing began to ease as she wiped her eyes with a sleeve.

"How?" she whispered sadly, "You heard what my Dad said. That's his main computer, the one that has everything for his business on. He hasn't got that information saved anywhere else. And if he can't get the information that he needs, then he can't quote a price for that big job he's been asked to cost up, and he won't get enough work for the factory for the winter, and he'll have to sack people and then he'll have to sell the house and then we'll have to live in a caravan, next to a donkey sanctuary and…"

"Ok, ok, I get the point!" Alex interrupted. He vigorously scratched his head and frowned. "If only we had stayed downstairs. If only we hadn't played on the computer."

"If only I hadn't pressed *'Delete All Files',"* Georgie added.

"If, if, if..." Alex continued.

"If only we could turn back time!" they both said out loud. Then they stopped, turned and stared at each other in silence for a few moments.

"You're not thinking what I'm thinking, are you?" asked Alex, first looking at his watch, then back up at his cousin again.

Georgie bit down hard on her lip again before nodding slowly. "I think I might be. But it was just a trick. Wasn't it?"

"Well now I think that there's only one way that we can really find out, isn't there?" Alex replied, adding, "Look, if we're lucky, we've probably got less than an hour before your parents come home. Come on, it's got to be worth a go, hasn't it?" Georgie looked doubtful, but then reluctantly nodded.

"But Alex, what if it doesn't work?" Georgie said quietly.

Alex smiled kindly. "Let's put it this way, we can always ask him if he knows how to fix computers first! We can't get into any more trouble that we're in already, can we?"

And so, with that, the two children sped down the stairs, stopping only to each put on a waterproof jacket, and ran out the front door, with a faint glimmer of hope in their hearts. Off in the direction of the one person in the village who could possibly save the day for them.

Chapter 5 – There and Back Again.

By the time that they'd reached Slipp Manor again, the clouds were dark and heavy, with thunder rumbling like a giant walking across the skies above them. Torrents of rain lashed down heavily around them, rebounding up from the ground, soaking any unprotected parts of their clothes. Alex pulled hard on the doorbell. He could hear the bell ring dimly inside the house. No reply. Alex bent down to peer through the letterbox, but Georgie pulled him back sharply.

"We've not got time to go through all that nonsense again!" she shouted, her voice almost being drowned out by another tremendous boom from the clouds that were continuing to grow angrier overhead.

"But he must be in, he must!" Alex answered desperately, quickly moving around the side of the house to find the kitchen window, peering intently through the shutters. Still there appeared to be no sign of Slipp, only the sight of some of the Kitty Clan, cowering under the kitchen table, eyes wide with fear, hiding from the storm.

"Alex! Quick, He's here!" Georgie screamed in delight as she too looked through a gap in one of the shutters that covered the windows to the living room. Alex ran back to join her, splashing through the puddles on the drive, ignoring the wetness that seeped into his trainers, squelching between his toes.

There, on the scruffy blue sofa that they had shared with him a matter of hours before, Slipp sat, dressed in a dressing gown, pyjamas and slippers. He appeared to be watching the television, Gizmo curled up fast asleep in his lap.

Frantically, the children pounded their fists on the shutter and began to shout. However, Slipp seemed not to notice them, continuing to sip occasionally from the large mug that he held in his hand.

"It's no good, he can't hear us with all the other racket that going on around us. Let's try and open this shutter so that we can get to the window itself." Georgie said, pulling on the wood. Alex nodded, water dripping from his fringe, as he joined in with her efforts.

It seemed to be pointless at first, but then, suddenly a rotten piece of shutter broke away in their hands, causing them to fall to the ground, water, wood and splinters flying everywhere around them. "YES!" they screamed in unison, as they quickly clambered back up and pulled the shutters wide apart, exposing the grimy, wet window before them.

Inside the house, Slipp was, indeed, blissfully unaware of the stormy drama unfolding outside. Having just got out of the bath, he was now enjoying a nice hot cup of tomato soup as he settled down to watch his favourite television programme, 'How History Happened.'

The last thing he could possibly have expected to hear was the loud banging and shouting that suddenly came from the window to the far right of him.

Bang. Bang. Bang! Bang! BANG!

"WAAAAAAAAAH!" he screamed, dropping his mug as he jumped up, out of his seat, spraying the last mouthful of the soup he had drunk out in front of him as he did so. Unfortunately, most of it hit the now airborne Gizmo, who only a moment before, slept peacefully on Slipp's lap, purring away happily. Now, he was flying like a furry cannonball! Despite spinning in mid-air, Gizmo was unable to land on all fours (no real surprise given his size). He gave out a large yelp as he fell to the floor in a crumpled heap, his grey and white fur now stained a fierce red, making him look like a sunburnt penguin!

Slipp turned toward the two wet faces that pressed and banged against the rain covered glass of the living room window.

"Lord Slipp! We need your help! Let us in! Please!" pleaded Alex and Georgie as Slipp raced out to the front door to let the two children in, his dressing gown opening like a superhero's cape behind him.

"Hurry now!" Slipp said as he ushered the two soggy children in, "Run into the kitchen and warm yourselves in front of the stove. I'll just go get you some towels to dry yourselves off or you'll both catch your death of colds!"

"No, we haven't got time," Georgie shouted, adding, "My Dad going to murder us both anyway if you can't help us, so it doesn't matter how wet we are!"

There, in the hallway, the three of them stood. Slipp listening intently, Alex and Georgie dripping and gesturing as they recounted the events of their disastrous encounter with the computer that afternoon.

Slipp frowned as he listened to the children finish their sorry tale. He paused for a moment, stroking the whiskers of his beard before he slowly, but surely, shook his head. "Oh dear, dear, dear." he repeated, whilst trying to wipe the soup from Gizmo's coat before the rest of the Kitty Clan summoned up the courage to appear from their hiding places all around Slipp Manor.

"So, you see, we were kind of hoping that you would know what to do about recovering the computer so that Dad won't know what we've done. Please!"

Georgie pleaded, yet again making her eyes look even bigger than they normally were.

Slipp sighed, putting Gizmo down. "Children, I would really love to help, but modern computer coding is not something that I really know a lot about, especially if it's one of the system programs that these new computers already come loaded with."

"But you must be able to do something?" Alex argued.

"If it was something I've invented or a program I'd written or designed myself, then yes, of course, I could, but nowadays some of the algorithms these coders use are so sophisticated that they are beyond even me. I still use the HTML script that I learned at school as a boy, always been good enough for me! I'm so very sorry about that" he said sadly.

Alex looked at Georgie and, turning slightly toward her, covered his mouth with his hand and muttered something so that Slipp couldn't quite hear. She nodded and sighed.

"Ok," Alex said, continuing, "so can we try and, er, skip back to a time before the computer crashed on us?"

Slipp's face momentarily brightened, before being replaced by a quizzical frown. "Well, of course, we could, but do you really want to time skip?"

The two children nodded enthusiastically, like a pair of bobble-headed dolls.

Slipp rubbed his chin again suspiciously. "Hmmm, but I got the impression, by the way you two couldn't wait to leave so quickly earlier, that you didn't like travelling on The Time Skipper at all!"

"It's not that we didn't like it," Georgie began hesitantly, "it's just that we didn't believe that we'd actually gone anywhere, let alone back in time and that you had, erm, well, sort of, um..."

"Sort of what?" Slipp asked, looking more confused than ever.

"What she's trying to say is that we thought you'd played a trick on us!" Alex interrupted, adding, "So we were wondering if you would just tell us if it was a trick or whether you could really take us back to just before we broke Uncle Jon's computer."

At first, Slipp appeared taken aback, but then he started to roar with laughter, startling the children, who looked on silently as the tears began to roll down Slipp's face. Finally, he replied, quelling his laughter, "Oh you poor, poor children, what a day you've had!" he heaved, "I'd never dream of trying to make fun of anyone or make them look foolish, especially two sweet children, such as you!" he chuckled, patting them both gently on their heads.

"You mean…?" Georgie began hopefully, "You'll help us?"

Slipp nodded in reply. "Come on, follow me. Let's try and sort out this little mess out for you, shall we?"

Alex and Georgie beamed broadly as the three of them turned from the hall, back toward the living room, followed closely by Gizmo, who was still trying to lick off the tomato soup that matted his fur.

As they entered the living room, the children noticed that what remaining daylight there was had almost disappeared, replaced by a brooding darkness caused by the storm that raged ferociously around them.

Closing the living room door, Slipp gestured to them to sit down, back in their original positions on the sofa. As Alex was about to take his seat, through the window, he caught sight of a large bolt of lightning zig-zagging across the sky in the far distance. He began to count until a loud thunderclap, like a rifle shot, boomed around them. The eye of the storm was moving ever closer.

"Now," Slipp began, "at approximately what time did all of your problems with the computer begin?"

Georgie, resting back into the sofa, shrugged her shoulders. "I am not really sure exactly, probably around five-ish?" she turned to her cousin. "Alex?"

Alex nodded in agreement. "Yeah, about then. We'd not been on the computer very long, that's for sure."

Slipp picked up the dark glasses that they'd worn previously, as well as the remote control, from the coffee table in front of them. He again handed a pair to each of them, placing his own atop his bald head, and looked closely at the digital display on the remote. "All right then," he said, adding, "if I aim to take you both back to about half past four, that should give you plenty enough time, don't you think?"

"But what if we bump into our past selves?" asked Alex. "What do I say to me about why there is two of me?"

Slipp smiled warmly. "Don't worry, trust me, all that's just the work of fiction. There is only one of you."

Georgie looked slightly confused. "Yes, now, but what about the 'then' me. Surely, we'd still be there, in the past?"

Slipp stretched his arms out wide, with both thumbs and forefingers pointing upwards and outwards. "Imagine that your timeline is like being in a queue." He began, moving his right thumb and forefinger along the imaginary line before him as he continued to explain.

"All we are doing is moving from the front of the queue to stand in a different position in it. It's a bit like jumping time zones when you go somewhere on holiday and you have to change your watch to the local time! As long as anything you say or do only affects you when you skip, then there's no harm done! Does that make more sense now?"

The two children nodded eagerly as Slipp added, "Good. After all, The Time Skipper is only meant to go back in minutes and hours! It's not like we're going to go back and try to save the dinosaurs!" he laughed as he began to key in some numbers on the remote control.

"1…6…3…0…Ent…oops, nearly forgot," Slipp said, reaching down and rummaging in between the cushions on the sofa, "I should have asked you to put these on last time. Can't be too careful now, can we?"

He produced a black safety belt and, drawing it across his lap, he clicked in the clasp on the opposite side of him, tugging it tightly to check it had caught securely.

Alex and Georgie reached down beside them, found their belts and started to fasten them too. Alex did his up straight away, but Georgie couldn't quite get it to click in its catch.

"Let me help you dear," said Slipp, passing the remote to Alex, "Would you hold this for a moment? Please don't press anything!"

"Yeah, no problems," Alex replied, carefully resting the control on the arm of the sofa next to him as Slipp leant over and started to adjust Georgie's safety belt.

"Sorry about this Georgie, we'll have this done in a jiffy," Slipp mumbled as he fumbled with the catch, "There. Done," he said as the lock snapped shut.

"Thank you," Georgie replied, checking that the belt was secure before putting her glasses on.

"Alex, please would you like to do the honours," asked Slip, sliding the dark glasses down from his head onto the bridge of his bony nose, covering his other glasses with them.   Settling back into his seat, he continued, "When you are ready, kindly press the ENTER button on the remote and remember to put your glasses on immediately!"

"Really? Wicked!" Alex exclaimed as he jabbed at the remote, took the glasses quickly from his lap and put them squarely over his eyes, ignoring the slight knot that was beginning to form in his stomach.

As before, after the initial silence, a loud whirring sound came from the black box as it kicked back into life. But, this time, it was joined with a brilliant flash of lightning that filled the room, along with a huge thunderclap from outside that caused the windowpane to shake in its frame. All of this proved to be too much for Gizmo, who unbeknown to them, was now sleeping contently beneath the coffee table as they prepared to depart in The Time Skipper. Terrified, he leapt up, landing on the remote control on the arm of the sofa, knocking it heavily into Alex's lap.

"Ouch! What on Earth was that?" Alex cried out, lifting his glasses, only to see the room around them start to spin, as though they were in a giant washing machine!

The room, furniture, ornaments, even colours, all began to merge into one, replaced by a fierce, burning, white light.

Frightened, Alex closed his eyes tightly shut as the brightness of the light hurt them, causing him to see little sun spots on the inside of his eyelids.

"Hold on tight, it'll be over in a few moments," Slipp shouted over the din, as the numbers on the black box's display flashed once, then twice, and then changed from red, through amber, to green before finally stopping.

'BEEP. BEEP. BEEP.' went the box, shrilly.

"Right. So, here we all are, safe and sound and back…" Slipp said

triumphantly, removing the dark glasses with a flourish.

"In a field!" Georgie shrieked after removing hers.

Indeed, there, stood behind the television in front of them, was a large dark

horse grazing happily away on the long grass that grew beside what looked

like a dirt path.

"What are we doing outside?" asked Alex, peering at Gizmo, who was

hanging onto the arm of the sofa next to him for dear life. Beyond the cat,

Alex could see a bridge crossing a river to a large town or city that he did not

recognise as being anything like Codswallop. "And where exactly are we?"

Slipp scratched his head repeatedly as he stared at the pleasant countryside

around him.   Slowly, he unbuckled his belt and went to stand up. "Most odd.

I'm not too sure, but we appear to have moved somewh-errrrrrrrrrroooomph!"

Slipp screamed as he slipped off the rug, scaring Gizmo even more! Alex and

Georgie looked briefly at each other in surprise, before looking down at their

feet. There Slipp lay, face down on the ground, about four feet beneath them,

his face planted in, and covered, by what looked like a large mud pie.

"It also looks like we have landed on top of something. Or someone."

Georgie cried, pointing at the feet that stuck out from under the sofa.

"Yes, you have, my father, Thomas Farriner, and his cart!" screamed a young

voice from behind them. They both turned and looked over the back of the

sofa to see a boy running toward them from behind a tall tree across the field.

He must have been around about thirteen or fourteen but was dressed quite

strangely in a white, loose fitting shirt, and brown, baggy trousers.

Slipp gingerly sat up and slowly began to wipe the brown goo from his face with his handkerchief, which, judging by the look on his face as he smelt it, was obviously not mud!

"We had just stopped so that I could have a pee when you appeared out of nowhere!" the boy said shakily, obviously in shock, "Please help me get my father out from under your...your, thing!"

Alex and Georgie clambered down and, between them, the four of them carefully lifted the Time Skipper and moved it gently down, to reveal the wooden cart that they had landed on, now titled to one side. One of its wheels had come off and lay on the ground next to it.

In the back of the cart lay the boy's father, wedged in a bed of what appeared to be a mixture of bread, pies and pastry. He was dressed just like the boy but wore a white cloth hat too.

"Don't worry, I'll call an ambulance." Georgie declared, grabbing her phone from her back pocket. She scrolled through her apps then frantically tapped the screen, getting more and more frustrated, her finger hitting the screen harder each time. "Just typical, no reception as usual!" she moaned as the boy ran to the man, shaking his shoulder, speaking loudly into his ear.

"Father, are you well?" he asked, shaking the man even harder. The man started to moan and twitched open his eyes.

"What happened, Tom?" he groaned as, helped by the boy, he groggily sat up, rubbing his head before exclaiming, "Look at my cart! And my wares! Who has done this foul deed?" The boy pointed to Slipp and the children, who now stood just to the side of the man.

"'Twas them, Father. They did it. Fell out of the sky in that strange craft of theirs!" Tom replied, pointing repeatedly at the Time Skipper.

67

"What strange manner of witchcraft is this?" the ruddy-faced man said as he shakily stood up, before climbing down from what was left of his cart. He walked purposely toward Slipp and, being much shorter, stood nose to chest with him.

Despite his lack of height, Farriner looked up fiercely at Slipp's face. "Well, what sayeth you, sir? Speak now, or I shall strike you squarely on the nose!" Slipp held his hands up in front of him and started to back away, slowly.

"I am most terribly sorry." he said, apologetically, "somehow we appear to have arrived somewhere other than we intended to."

He pointed at the damaged cart and smiled nervously. "Please, let us help you so that we can all be on our way with no harm. But, before we do, can you tell us exactly how far we are from Codswallop?"

The man looked less angry but more confused. "Codswallop? Codswallop is what you're talking more like! There's no place called Codswallop that I know of near London, and I've lived here all my life, man and boy!"

"London! What in heaven's name are we doing here?" Slipp gasped, sitting in a heap back on the ground, holding his head in his hands. Gizmo, having bravely climbed down from the sofa, walked up to him, sniffed his face and then quickly ran away, coughing and spluttering in disgust!

The man shook his head, then smiled and sighed. "Aside from wrecking my cart, I have no idea!" He extended a hand to help Slipp up. "Thomas Farriner, Master Baker to the King and his Royal Navy. And this here be my young son Tom," he added, nodding toward the boy, who was busy looking around the Time Skipper with both Alex and Georgie.

Slipp stood up and shook his hand. "Lord Thyme-Slipp, here's my card, and these are my friends, Alex and Georgie." Farriner looked at the card Slipp had given him and scratched his head as Slipp continued speaking, "Baker to the King's Royal Navy? Surely you must mean the Queen's?"

Farriner shook his head as he smiled broadly. "No, King Charles of course!"

Slipp's eyes bulged as he gasped. "Charles? That's impossible. Queen Elizabeth rules England, not Charles!"

"Elizabeth? Her reign ended some sixty years ago, King Charles has ruled England for over thirty years." Farriner said, looking puzzled, "You really ain't from round here, are you?"

Slipp shook his head, standing once more. "No, we most definitely are not! It would appear that we have travelled far through time and space, into the future!" he said, dramatically pointing up to the stars, holding his pose for a second for greater effect.

Overhearing what he'd said, Alex called from behind the two men. "Lord Slipp, I don't know if this will help," Alex stated, continuing, "but I think that you'd better come look at this!" Slipp frowned as he turned and bounded over to Alex who was knelt in front of the black box under the television. "Look!" Slipp began to look at the display but then removed his glasses, cleaned them before returning to look at the display again. On it, the numbers '1-6-6-6' flashed away brightly in green. "That's odd, I don't understand why -."

Then a look of horror and understanding crept over his face.

"What does it mean, Lord Slipp?" Alex asked, but Slipp didn't hear him, calling back over to Farriner instead.

"You did say King Charles, didn't you Master Farriner?"

Farriner, who was still examining his cart closely, sighed before answering loudly. "Yes. Charles the Second, it is his court who I serve as Conduct of the King's Bakehouse. Now, would someone please tell me what is going on here?"

Slipp suddenly squatted down, put his head back into his hands, and, shaking it slowly, started to rock gently from side to side.

"What's the matter?" Georgie asked worriedly as she came over to join them.

Slipp continued to rock in silence, like the pendulum of a clock.

It was Alex who spoke first. "Slipp thinks that we may have accidentally travelled forward through space and time."

Georgie looked taken aback by the news, the colour draining from her face.

"Just exactly how far have we gone? Are my mum and dad home, because if they are then we're for it?"

"I don't think we'd need worry about that Georgie. You see, I've a funny feeling that's the least of our problems," Alex whispered quietly so that Tom, who was now sat on the sofa stroking Gizmo, could not hear. Georgie looked even more worried as he continued, "I don't think we are in the future, are we Lord Slipp?"

On hearing his name, Slipp, as though waking from a dream, stopped rocking and slowly looked up at the two children. "No, sadly not," he sighed, adding, "If my memory serves me right, I think we've probably travelled back over 350 years in the past!"

Chapter 6 – The Streets of London.

The three of them stood, open-mouthed, looking at one another as the truth finally dawned on them. It was Farriner who broke the uneasy silence by calling to them as he tried to right his cart and salvage its contents.

"Well? Spit it out. What have you been talking about over there?" he asked, a little more firmly this time.

"Lord Slipp was just telling us how he thought that we may have trav - humph!" Georgie went to reply, only for her words to be cut off by Slipp's hand gently covering her mouth, acting like a muffler!

"Nothing for you to worry about!" shouted Slipp in reply, waving toward Farriner and Tom with his free hand, "We'll be over in just a moment to explain and offer you our help." He turned to Georgie, her big eyes staring crossly back at him over the top of his fingers. Slipp put his index finger to his lips and began to speak in hushed tones. "Georgie, we can't tell them we're time travellers, they wouldn't possibly believe us or even begin to understand," he whispered as he leant closely into her, "This is England during the Middle Ages, after all."

"Yeah, they might burn us at the stake like witches!" Alex added quietly through the corner of his mouth. Georgie's eyes bulged in surprise as she gulped loudly. Slipp nodded in agreement as he carefully took his hand away from her mouth when he was quite sure that she had calmed down.

"But how on Earth did we end up here?" Georgie asked softly.

Slipp scratched his chin. "I'm not altogether sure. It might have had something to do with the thunderstorm. Lightning strikes can cause chaos to electronic equipment and devices. Add that to the fact that I was watching the Historical Channel before we time skipped could be why we've been propelled here! It could be any number of factors, I just don't know at this point. Without being at home to properly diagnose it, I can only speculate," Slipp frowned, "Anyway, it doesn't matter now. It's best we don't talk about it, too many ears, if you know what I mean." Alex and Georgie both nodded eagerly in agreement. "It's vital that we don't frighten these people if we are to have any hope of returning home safely."

"So, what say you?" Farriner shouted, even more urgently this time. Slipp walked over toward the baker before putting an arm around his shoulders. "What little Georgie was about to say was that we have travelled many, many miles to reach London, travelling great distances from, er, from, erm -."

"Arabia!" Alex blurted out, wildly, pointing to the rug, before adding, "On our magic carpet!"

"Brilliant!" exclaimed Slipp, "I mean, yes, on our magic carpet! We have travelled here across deserts and mountains, passing over many oceans, to visit your fine country," he declared, sweeping his hand theatrically across the landscape.

At first, Farriner looked sceptical and confused, as though seeing through the lie. But then he began to slowly nod, a look of recognition filling his ruddy face. "Yes, yes, I do seem to recall such tales told of eastern wonders by a French nobleman at one of the King's banquets. You remember that don't you, Tom?"

Tom emerged from under the cart, his eyes appearing to light up at the memory. "Yes, that I do! They were such wonderful tales of mystery and adventure. The man said that he'd heard stories told in coffee houses, of carpets that magically flew, whilst travelling through Persia and Egypt. Farriner and Tom began to look intently at the rug, prodding it gently with their feet, as though scared of the power contained within it. Unseen behind them, Slipp gave a big thumbs up toward Alex, who bowed in return, pleased with his deceit.

"Never thought that I'd be fortunate enough to see one with my own eyes, especially with such exotic seating!" Farriner said, pointing at the sofa that sat atop the tatty old rug.

"Now, well, you see, this is not just any old carpet. Oh, no sire! This is the great sultan Aladdin's very own magic carpet." Slipp said proudly, clapping his hands by the side of his head, as though summoning someone or something. Farriner and Tom both looked blankly at him, paying no attention to the name. "Aladdin? Princess Jasmine? Jafar? Lamp? Genie? Anybody?" They shook their heads as Slipp sighed, deflatedly. "No? Ah well, never mind. I suppose we have far more pressing matters to attend to."

"I'll say," Farriner replied, before adding, "like explaining to his majesty as to why I am unable to deliver all of this for the great banquet tomorrow" he swept his arm over the back of the cart, "We were off to deliver our first batch of bread and pastries when you landed on us. Serves me right for changing my usual delivery plans!"

"What do you mean?" Alex asked as he and Tom began to lift the missing wheel that lay on the ground near them.

"Normally we load our cart up from the bakery and ride through the city to deliver to the royal palace in Whitehall," Tom said, pointing back over his shoulder with his free hand across the river toward London, "But my father decided that today, because of the amount of food we were taking, that it would be easier to travel on this side of the riverbank through St. George's Fields instead."

"Why?" Georgie asked as she poked her finger into one on the loaves. She pulled a huge chunk of bread and gave some to Gizmo, before tasting it herself. "Oh, my god, that's so yummy!"

Farriner smiled at her as he shook his head. "To stop the likes of you my girl stealing food off the cart from us. There are lots of hungry peasants on the streets of London. Tom and I were travelling this way as there as fewer houses and people on this side of the river. We were then going to load our goods onto my brother's boat, which is moored near where he lives not far from here. Then we were to row it across the Thames to meet with my manservant, Teagh, and our other cart on the other side of the water. It's then just a short journey to the palace with far fewer peasants to pass by." He sighed, pointing further down the river from them. "It was meant to be a much simpler, stress-free journey! Well, so much for that bright idea! I'll have to go back and start baking all over again, that's if I can get my cart fixed of course!"

"I'm so very sorry. Look, the very least that we can do is to help you get home again." Slipp replied, apologetically, looking closely at the damaged cart, "I don't think it'll prove too difficult for us to repair, not if we all work together. It appears to have just come apart than being totally wrecked, so that's a positive! If Master Farriner and I lift it up on this side that will allow Tom and

Alex to roll the wheel back into position. Then Georgie can slip the wooden pin back into the axle, and we can use a little brute force to wedge it back in place. Agreed?" Everyone nodded, the general mood lifting for all of them as they moved to their agreed positions. "All right, so on the count of three then. One, two, three. Heave!"

Farriner and Slipp lifted the cart off the ground, grunting as they bore its weight. Alex and Tom quickly rolled the wheel over beside it and slotted the axle through the hole in the middle of it.

Georgie looked around on the ground, found the pin and slotted it into back into place. Then Farriner and Slipp let go of the cart and Tom hit the pin repeatedly with a large rock he had found, making sure that it was firmly in place.

"There!" He said in triumph, as the cart stood upright again before them. "It's as good as new, Father!"

Farriner looked at what remained of his produce. "If only the same could be said of these," he said sadly, picking up a loaf that now looked more like a pancake! Tom ran to fetch their horse, who hadn't strayed far from them and was still munching happily away on the grass, before bringing him back and tethering him to the front of their cart. Farriner patted the horse gently, reassuring him, before turning to Slipp and the children again.

"Thank you for your help in fixing the cart, but we must be away now. We now have many more hours of baking to do to replace all of this, so we must make haste. Come, Tom, let us be off."

"Farewell to you all." Tom waved as they led the horse, turning him, and the cart, around back in the direction of the bridge.

Slipp, Alex and Georgie looked on as they slowly trudged away. "Surely there's something we can do to help? After all, it was our fault." Georgie asked, guiltily.

Slipp thought for a moment. "Wait! Master Farriner, let us come with you. We can have a Great British bake off!" he shouted, running after them.

"Seriously?" groaned Alex, "If they haven't heard of Aladdin, what chance have you got with that?!"

Farriner turned and smiled. "Really, that would be most kind of you. As John Heywood once said, 'many hands make light work!' But what will we do with your magic carpet? We have no room to carry it on our cart, let alone house such a fine craft in my yard."

"Why don't we just fly it there?" Tom asked, his eyes lighting up at the prospect.

"Probably not a good idea," Slipp replied, "we wouldn't want to frighten anyone, would we, it's quite a sight when she's in full flight!"

Slipp hated to see the disappointment in Tom's face, but the truth was that the Time Skipper was only supposed to travel in time. There was no way of making it change locations, not that he was aware of anyway. Today had been an odd fluke. Or so he hoped.

Tom smiled and nodded. "Not to worry. Master Slipp, I understand."

Slipp smiled back, looking around him. "Tell you what, let's move it behind that copse over there, out of harm's way," he said, pointing to a small clump of trees, "By the looks of it, it'll be quite safe there for a few hours."

After fifteen minutes of furious activity, the Time Skipper was completely hidden from view, covered by a vast array of branches, twigs and leaves. The five of them stood back and admired their work, satisfied that it was safe for them to leave.

So, with the remote control being tucked safely in Slipp's dressing gown pocket, they all set off toward London Bridge. Slipp and Farriner led the horse and cart, chatting easily to one another, like life-long friends. Tom, Alex and Georgie sat at the front of the cart, taking it in turns to hold the reins. Last, but by no means least, was Gizmo, full, fat and content from eating too much bread, snoring soundly, fast asleep in the back.

It wasn't too long before they reached the bridge itself, passing unchallenged through a gatehouse at its entrance. Alex and Georgie gazed around them in wonder as they crossed it. Boats filled the river Thames on either side, fishing boats, row boats and a tall ship bobbing about on the water. Alex noticed that the bridge was made from large stone blocks forming about 20 irregularly spaced arches that were set into the river-bed. It was wide enough, he reckoned, so that five carts could travel side by side along its length, which must have been at least a thousand feet, judging by the size of the buildings that appeared in the distance. In the middle of the bridge was a drawbridge which appeared to be regularly used to allow the tall ships to pass beneath the bridge as they travelled along the Thames.

Up ahead of them, the tall wooden buildings that filled the streets of London started to grow as they moved toward them, bringing them closer into view. Upon passing through the second gatehouse, they immediately entered London itself, with the sounds of the city suddenly filling the air, a shock to their ears after the peace and quiet of the river crossing. The children gasped, amazed at how close together the rickety wooden houses were built.

People bustled and jostled about, knocking and bumping each other as they went on their way. In some of the side streets, neighbours were almost able to shake hands with one another through their upstairs windows, so narrow was the space between them. Alex looked down at the cobbled road as the cart's wheels rolled over them, and was amazed to see that they were covered in litter and mucky water. He held his nose tightly, almost gagging at the smell that filled the air around them.

"Urgh! Why does it stink so much?" He asked as they moved further along the windy streets.

"That'd be the slops!" Tom replied as they passed so close to one building that they could see the people inside eating together.

"What on Earth are slops?" Georgie asked, waving her hand in front of her nose as though shooing the smell away.

Slipp turned back at them and smiled. He held his dressing gown sleeve up close to his nose, muffling the sound of his voice.

"Ah, yes, well you see, they don't have indoor plumbing or toilets like we do in, er, Arabia," he winked knowingly,

"So, what do they have instead?" asked Georgie, this time pulling the neck of her top up high over her nose and mouth.

"Buckets my dear!" Slipp replied, laughing at the disgusted looks on both Alex and Georgie's young faces.

"Ew, that's so gross!" Georgie replied, looking slightly paler than usual.

Alex looked like he was going to throw up. "Then what do they do with it afterwards?" He wasn't sure that he really wanted to know the answer, but curiosity got the better of him.

"Well, usually they'd just empty them out of the windows, into the streets below," answered Slipp as Tom pointed up to a wrinkly old woman, who was leaning out of her window, with a wooden bucket in one hand.

"Like she be doing," said Tom as Slipp, Alex and Georgie looked up, just in time to see the woman tip up the bucket, emptying its contents down into the street below.

"Mind it don't hit yo -." Farriner began to say, leading the horse slightly to the right, just as the brownie coloured liquid drenched Slipp from head to foot!!

"I think I'm going to be sick!" gagged Alex, putting both hands across his mouth, struggling hard not to retch.

"Not half as sick as he must be feeling," Georgie replied, pointing at Slipp, who stood there, dripping like a wet flannel! Potato skins hung from his nose, whilst carrot and turnip tops rested on his head and shoulders. He gingerly sniffed his shirt and, looking relieved, sighed.

"Fortunately, looks like it was only dinner peelings! Trust me, it could have been much, much worse!" he laughed, brushing himself down, before continuing to walk the cart, his slippers squelching as they pounded the cobblestones. They had only travelled a few more metres before Farriner turned and led the horse and cart into a small yard, set a little way back from the street, with houses hemming it in on all sides.

"Well, here we are, home sweet home!" Farriner said as they entered the yard. Slipp and the children all failed to notice the battered old wooden sign that hung outside the gates of the yard.   It read *'Thomas Farriner Esq. Master Baker. Fish Yard, Pudding Lane.'*

Chapter 7 – Ready Steady Cooks!

"Hannah? Alice?" Farriner called out as they entered the large bakery at the back of the yard. There were five large brick ovens, with kindle wood under each. "We're home and have brought guests with us!" he cried, waving everybody in.

A young, plain, slight woman, carrying a small child, came down the stairs at the end of the room and smiled warmly at them.

"Allow me to introduce my beautiful daughter, Hannah, and her little sister Mary," beamed Farriner proudly, continuing, "Hannah, where's Alice?

"Alice has taken to bed with one of her headaches again, Father. We may need to think about getting another maid," Hannah replied shaking her head.

"Not to worry," Farriner sighed, "anyway, I've bought some new friends for you to meet who *bumped* into us on our travels today!"

"Pleased to meet you all," Hannah said, looking slightly confused, "You must be parched. Would you like something to quench your thirst?" she asked, carefully placing her sister down on the floor. The toddler held a large piece of bread in her hand and munched happily away on it.

"Yes, please!" almost everyone answered at once as Hannah went away to fetch some drinks. Farriner went to a room at the side of the bakery and opened the door which led to a storeroom. He leant in slightly, looking around at its contents.

"Good. It looks like we'll have enough to be getting on with in here. Tom, if you could get everything that we need out ready for us. We'll then need to clear out the cart in preparation for the next load that we produce. I fear that it's going to be a long and busy night," he said sadly, only for his face to brighten as his daughter came back into the room. In her hands, she carried a tray full of wooden goblets, each filled to the brim and carefully handed a drink in turn to everyone.

"Ah, mead! Drink of the ancients. Nectar of the Gods!" Slipp said triumphantly, tasting the sweet drink. Everyone else stopped and looked at him strangely.

"If you don't mind me saying Alex, but your master is a little odd!" whispered Tom, as Slipp smacked his lips again after taking a second sip.

"No, he's a lot odd!" Alex laughed, drinking from his goblet.

"Master Slipp, it's called Small Mead," Hannah said cheerfully, "we can't be letting the young ones get drunk on the proper stuff, can we now?!"

Alex and Georgie looked at each other disappointedly before continuing to thirstily drink the mead.

"What are you going to do with all of the leftovers in your cart Master Farriner?" Georgie asked in-between mouthfuls.

Farriner shook his head. "Nowt else to do but throw it away, they are no good to neither man nor beast I'm afraid."

"But you must be able to do something with them," Slipp asked, hiccupping slightly as he did so.

Farriner thought for a moment then again shook his head. "No, nothing that springs to mind."

"Surely, we can make bread and butter pudding, or use some of the bread as pizza bases or something?" Alex suggested. All the Farriners looked at him blankly as though he'd spoken in a different language to them.

"I confess I have heard of the pudding that you mention, though not this *peetzer*?" replied Farriner, "You know of them both?" Slipp and the two children nodded eagerly as he continued, "Would you show us how to make them?"

"We would be most delighted to!" Slipp replied, grabbing a cloth apron from an old wooden table at the side of the room, "Now children, run along and gather up as much of the bread from the cart as you can. Be sure that it has no, ahem, little extras in it! Master Farriner, you continue making your replacement food and we will prepare and make these wonderful new dishes for you. They'll be the talk of the royal court!"

With that, Alex and Georgie ran to the cart and fetched as much of the food as could be saved, or hadn't been destroyed, or which didn't have any of Gizmo's dribbly teeth marks or fur in! Gizmo snorted his disapproval at being woken as they moved him gently, before collecting the bread and returning to the kitchen.

By the time they got back, Farriner had set a light under the wood beneath each of his ovens and had begun to mix the ingredients that Tom was providing from the storeroom.

"Excellent, excellent!" Slipp commented as he spread the children's haul on his part of the table. He began to butter some of the wheat bread and added whatever bits of fruit he himself had found in Farriner's storeroom. "I wasn't able to find any sultanas or milk, so I am having to use bits of pear, oranges and almond milk," he whispered to the children as he brushed some honey over the top of the bread and butter pudding, "There's no sugar in England yet either, so I've had to use a little honey instead!"

"And people eat this muck?" Farriner said after Slipp had passed the completed dish to him.

"Yes, but you do have to cook it first!"

Farriner, looking at it sceptically, placed the dish into the furthermost oven. Hannah picked up Mary, who had been happily gurgling away on the floor, and turned for the stairs. "Think I'd better get you out of harm's way, Mary," she said, adding, "Would you like to come with us, Georgie? Let's leave the men here to get on with their work?"

"Thought that you'd never ask!" Georgie replied as she sped up the stairs like a demented greyhound. "Give me a shout when you've finished boys, there are some advantages to being a girl in the middle ages after all!" she called out, her laughter echoing back down the stairs as she did so.

"Blooming' cheek!" replied Alex, dumping the last load of bread, which were the flattest, most misshapen pieces left at bottom of the cart, onto the table. Slipp made sure that each piece was as flat as it could be by sitting on top of it, a loaf positioned beneath each buttock!

"Remind me not to try a piece!" laughed Tom as Slipp continued bouncing up and down on the hard surface like it was a bouncy castle!

At last, he finally stopped, and wiping a bead of sweat from his brow, turned to the baker, who had been trying to concentrate on his own replacement pastries and pies nearby.

"Now, do you have any meat, vegetables or fruit lying around that we can place on top of these?" Slipp asked, gesturing towards his bottom-shaped bread bases.

Farriner looked up, flour covered his arms and face. "Er, what do you need?"

"Oh, some mushrooms, onions, peppers, tomatoes, ham, cheese, pork, beef, children…," Slipp replied.

"Children!" exclaimed Tom and Alex anxiously.

"Oops, sorry, meant chicken!" laughed Slipp. Tom and Alex sighed in relief. It had been a strange day after all.

"Tom, go and see what you can find for us" Tom began to walk toward the storeroom as his master continued "I think we have most of what you need but, I must confess, I know not what these *tomatoes* are."

"They're small, red, round and juicy, usually grown on a vine," said Alex, his stomach rumbling again at the very thought of food.

"Ah, you must mean *Love Apples!*" Farriner answered.

"Er, yeah, whatever," Alex replied, not really concentrating on anything other than the smell of the food now cooking in the various ovens.

"Love apples?" asked Slipp, "That's a name I've not heard them called before."

"Well, that's what Sir Walter Raleigh called them when he returned from his travels. I think that we may have a few of them somewhere here, one of the perks of working for the court of the king, the plentiful supply of exotic foods and ingredients!"

Farriner raced off after Tom. When he was safely out of earshot, Alex whispered to Slipp.

"So, when are we going to go home?" he asked, "Our parents are going to be so worried about us when they get back and find us not there." Slipp ruffled Alex's hair, gently, much to his annoyance.

"You're not to worry. Our time's frozen whilst we're here. The clock will start ticking again the moment we get back. They'll never know that we've been away if we plan the moment of our return carefully. We'll just help them finish their baking and we'll be on our way. It's the least we can do." Just then, Tom and Farriner returned, arms full.

"Well, we have ham, mushrooms, pork, cheese, apples, onions, beans and love app-, I mean tomatoes. Will that do?"

"Splendid!" Slipp replied happily, clapping his hands loudly.

It wasn't too long before he was frantically chopping up the ingredients he'd been given. Alex mashed up the tomatoes in a small stone bowl, before spreading the red paste he'd made over all the bread bases Slipp had laid out. Farriner and Tom watched on in amazement, scarcely believing their eyes at the sight that lay before then.

Just then, there came a loud banging sound from the bakery door. Tom raced to open it and there, silhouetted in the doorway, stood a tall, thin well-dressed man. His face was as pale as the white, powdery wig that he wore, with a tall hat carefully balanced on top of that. He entered the room, barely acknowledging Tom as he passed him.

"Good day Farriner," he said snootily, as he moved further into the bakery, swinging a walking cane before him.

"Good afternoon, Sir Granville," answered Farriner worriedly, "To what do we owe this unexpected pleasure?"

Sir Granville-Greville looked down his nose as he walked around the bakers, as though disgusted to be there. He produced a handkerchief from his sleeve and dabbed it under his nostrils. "I have come directly from the Palace having spoken with your manservant, Teagh, who awaits you there still. Were we not to receive our first delivery this afternoon for the great banquet tomorrow?"

"Yes, you were, but…" Farriner began.

"No *'buts'*, Farriner!" Sir Granville said angrily, his face colouring, going from a deathly white to a pinkish hue, "Failure to meet your duty and order will have grave consequences for you and your family. Remember this, there are many that wish to be appointed the Royal Baker. Tomorrow is a very important day for his majesty. I trust that you will not cause the King to doubt the faith he, unwisely, places in you after your service to the navy during the wars with the Dutch."

Before Farriner could respond, Slipp stepped forward to interrupt.

"Sir Granville, allow me to introduce myself. I am Lord Thyme-Slipp of the Codswallop Thyme-Slipps. My card," he said, producing a pig-eared, bread covered card from his dressing gown pocket before handing it to him, "It is an honour to meet a man of such high standing. My good friend Thomas has been kind enough to help me regarding my daughter Lady, er, erm …"

"Gizmo!" Alex piped up. Outside, they heard a loud 'Meooooow" and the sound of claws scraping against wood as the cat tried to get down off the cart at the sound of his name.

"Brilliant! Er, yes, it is my only daughter Gizmo's 21st birthday. She is a comely looking wench, and would make someone a very fine wife!" Slipp stepped closer to Sir Granville, "Tell me, Sir Granville, are you married?" he asked, placing an arm around Sir Granville's shoulders as he casually turned him around, back toward the door.

"Er, well, actually, no I never found the right –" Sir Granville stuttered, his cheeks flushing at the flattery.

"Oh really, I am most surprised at that. Well then you must come to the party, I'll introduce the two of you. I must confess, she is the cat's whiskers, if I do say so myself! I've a feeling that she will practically purr with delight were

she to meet you! Anyway, must dash. I must help Thomas complete his

order after taking up so much of his time arranging my daughter's forthcoming

festivities. We'll make our first delivery to the Palace later this evening. Good

day Sir Granville, I look forward to seeing you again, very soon!"

And with that, Slipp pushed Sir Granville out through the door, closing it

quickly behind him. Sir Granville nearly tripped over the crumb-covered cat

that staggered past him in the yard.

"Hmm. Lady Gizmo Granville-Greville? I jolly well like the sound of that!" he

chuckled to himself. Dusting the flour from his shoulders, he strode out of the

yard onto the street, whistling happily, tapping his cane on the cobbles as he

walked.

The raucous laughter that burst out inside the bakery caused Georgie to run

downstairs from where she'd been playing with Mary.

"What on Earth's been going on down here?" she asked as she saw the men

and the boys laughing uncontrollably.

"Oh, we've just had to gently put someone in their place!" Slipp giggled,

adding, "We'll tell you all about it later, but first we must make haste! We

have a banquet to prepare for."

Everyone cheered as they frantically continued the cooking. Flour, water,

fruit, vegetables and various other ingredients flew from hand, to table, to pan

as bread, pizzas, pastries and pies were mixed, shaped, glazed and baked.

Such was the fury with which they all worked that nobody noticed that Gizmo

had crept in through an open window and curled up in a nice, warm, large pan

under the table, falling fast asleep yet again. Had Georgie not heard a loud '*sniff*' come from under the pastry lid that now covered the pot when carrying it toward one of the raging ovens, then the King would have been treated to a moggy-filled pie!

Finally, when the last oven had been filled, they were done. Farriner and Slipp collapsed against one another on a couple of stools. Georgie was slumped against the bakery wall, the stonework cooling her sweat-covered back whilst Alex and Tom lay flat-out on the cold, flour-covered floor. There, on the table before them, was a result of all their hard work.

"What a feast of food, Master Farriner!" Slipp exclaimed, patting his friend gently on the back.

Farriner, smiling tiredly, drew his arm across his brow, wiping away the sweat and the grime from the day. "Thank you all ever so much for all your help. The last of today's food should be ready within the hour, then I can transport it to the Palace and leave it with Teagh to look after overnight," he sighed, "All I'll have to do then is start on the next batch when I return, ready for the second delivery early tomorrow morning," he looked across at Tom, "Are you ready to load up and depart son?"

Tom, slowly sitting up, was about to answer, when Slipp intervened. "Why don't I come with you? That way, I can drive the cart whilst you relax next to me. Tom can stay here and have a break before he helps you bake the rest." Farriner thought for a moment before nodding. "An excellent idea. Come on let's get the cart loaded and be on our way. However, I would like to keep back some of that bread & butter pudding and *peetzer* to try. Perhaps you would like to share supper with us when we return?"

Before Slipp could reply, Alex and Georgie had jumped in. "Yes please, Master Farriner!" shouted Alex, adding, "It feels like I haven't eaten in years!"

"Over three hundred of them, to be exact!" laughed Georgie. They then all formed a line from table, to door, to cart and passed bread, pies, pizzas and pastries along their human chain to save time loading.

Soon the cart was full, the smell of the freshly cooked food making their mouths drool, and stomachs rumble as Farriner covered its contents with a large, brown sackcloth. He climbed up onto the front of the cart, with Slipp taking the reins beside him.

"I'll take no chances this time," he laughed, continuing, "we'll ride this side of the river to Whitehall Palace! Georgie, would you please fetch Hannah and help her to prepare a table for us all to sup from when we return. Also, see if the two of you can raise that lazy maid of ours from her sick bed too!?" he asked kindly. Georgie nodded and went inside. Alex and Tom stayed in the yard to wave Slipp and Farriner off, the horses' hooves clacking against the cobbles as they carefully made their way out through the gateway to begin their journey.

"I can't wait to see the Palace, I've so many questions I want to ask..." they heard Slipp say cheerfully, his voice becoming more distant as the cart rolled away toward the setting sun.

Chapter 8 – An Orange Crush.

The two boys stood silently for a moment before Alex turned to Tom. "So, what shall we do now?" he asked. Tom shrugged his shoulders and scratched his head.

"I suppose we had better go in and help tidy up and set supper," replied Tom.

"What! More work! Haven't we done enough for a bit? Can't we play out in the yard or something for a while?" Alex protested.

Tom thought for a moment before grinning. "I expect it wouldn't hurt if we took a minute or two, just to catch our breaths!" he said with a wink.

"Good man!" smiled Alex, "Have you got anything that we can play without here?"

Tom frowned and shook his head. "I work here, usually there's no time to play!"

As the two of them discussed what they might do, a young, pretty, teenaged girl, hair tightly curled in ringlets, walked past the entrance to the yard, basket in hand. Recognising her, Tom called out, "Nell! Wait up," and ran, chasing after her, Alex following closely behind. The girl had stopped and was now stood waiting on the street outside.

"Tom Farriner, as I live and breathe! You're looking as handsome as ever!" the girl smiled as Tom and Alex approached her, "Not seen you for a while. How's you been?"

Tom blushed a deep red. "I thought that you might have forgotten about your old friends, Nell, now that you're a famous actress and all?"

"How could I ever forget a fine friend like you, Tom?" Nell replied, planting a large kiss on his cheek, causing Tom to now look like a beetroot!

"So, tell me, who's this lovely young man? I ain't seen him around these parts?" Nell asked, turning her gaze in Alex's direction. It was now his turn to feel flustered.

Nevertheless, he stood up as straight as he could, making himself look as tall as possible. He stuck out a hand to introduce himself. "Hi. I'm Alex. Alex McClellan."

"Pleased to meet you, Alex-Alex McClellan! I'm Nell Gwynne, " she said, smiling, shaking him firmly by the hand, "Now then, what are you two up to? No good, no doubt, if I know my Tom!" If Tom had gone any redder his head would have exploded!

"No," Alex replied, "we were just about to play outside whilst waiting for, our, er, masters to return. Then we can have supper. Hope it's soon as we're starving!"

"Yes, we've been working so hard today!" Tom said, "Want to stay with us a while, Nell?"

Nell shook her head sadly. "I'd love to, but me ma's expecting me back home soon but, hang on a moment…" she said, rummaging around in her basket.

"Here you go! These ought to keep you going 'til supper time!" Nell tossed a couple of large oranges up in the air toward them both.

"Thought that you'd have had enough of these, Nell!" Tom laughed, biting into the rind of the orange he'd caught.

Nell just grinned. "Never. Anyway, best be on me way. Was a pleasure to meet you, Alex-Alex McClellan," she smiled, as she turned, waved and danced off down the street, singing away happily to herself.

The two boys stood and waved until she had disappeared from their view before they turned back into the yard.

There, on the far side of it, sat Gizmo, crouched low to the ground, her tail sweeping behind her. She had cornered a small brown mouse and was staring at it intently, making ready to pounce. Suddenly, without warning, the mouse squeaked loudly and moved forwards sharply, terrifying Gizmo. The startled cat jumped high, twisted in mid-air and landed about five feet away from the mouse. Gizmo quickly ran and hid behind the well that stood in the far corner of the yard, shaking nervously as the mouse scurried away triumphantly.

"Don't you want that?" Tom asked, pointing at the untouched orange that still sat in his friend's hand. Alex shook his head.

"Nah, I don't really like them that much. Plus, this one's a bit hard anyway," he replied, dropping the orange onto his knee, then flicked it back up in the air, before catching it again with his opposite hand.

Tom stood there open-mouthed before clapping wildly. "That was really good! Got any more tricks?"

"Sure," said Alex boastfully, "that was nothing. Just watch this!" With that, he juggled the orange repeatedly, first with his right foot, then his left, then both. Next, he flicked it up again, caught it on the back of his neck, before tossing it back up towards the sky and then, finally, caught it with one hand behind his back.

Tom cheered and whistled loudly.

"That's amazing! You should be up on the stage like Nell, doing those kinds of juggling tricks!"

Alex nonchalantly shrugged his shoulders. "Nah, there are much better players than me at footy."

Tom looked blankly back at him and shook his head. "Footy? What is footy?"

Alex looked at him in amazement. "Footy? Football?" Again, Tom shook his head so Alex continued, "You mean; you've never, ever played football?"

"No, nor heard of it," replied Tom, "can you teach me?" Alex nodded, before squatting down, looking closely at the ground.

"Ah, here we are," he said, picking a large white stone from the floor. He walked to one of the walls and started to draw on it with the stone.

"What are you doing?" Tom asked as Alex first drew a line up, then a line across, and finally, a line down the wall. He then took Tom's arm and, pointing at the wall, led him toward it.

"This is called a goal. You are the goalkeeper and stand here. I will go over there, put the orange on the ground and kick it at the goal. You must stop it from hitting the wall in between the drawn lines. If you don't, I get a goal and win. You save it, you win. Got it?"

Tom frowned and nodded. "I think so." He said as Alex placed the orange on a white spot that he'd also marked on the ground. He walked away from Tom, turned and sprinted back, before kicking the orange as hard as he could into the bottom of the chalk goal, it flying past Tom, hitting the wall before he could even begin to move.

"You're not singing anymore! You're not sing-ing any-more!" Alex sang loudly as he started dabbing and running around the yard. He then pulled his top up over his head and stuck his arms out beside him like an aeroplane's wings!

"But I wasn't singing in the first place!" Tom argued, looking slightly confused.

Alex pulled his top back down and walked up to Tom, placing a hand reassuringly on his shoulder.

"You geddit?" Alex asked, tossing the battered orange toward him. Tom nodded. "Good! Your turn," he added, jogging to take his place in the goal.

Tom carefully placed the orange on the ground, stepped back five paces, before running as fast as he could towards the orange. As he kicked it, his shoe flew off, narrowly missing Gizmo, who had poked his head around the well to see whether the mouse was still looking for him. On seeing the shoe flying toward him, he retreated with a yelp back into his hiding place! The orange, alas, had no such escape, exploding against the wall, despite Alex's best efforts to save it.

Flesh, pith, peel and pips exploded everywhere, showering Alex and the on-rushing Tom. The two boys laughed happily as they wiped themselves down, ignoring the stains the orange had created.

"Well, it looks like our game of foody's over then," said Tom, sadly.

"It's footy!" Alex corrected, "Yeah, probably, unless you've got anything else that's round enough for us to use instead?"

"Wait here," replied Tom, quickly running indoors. He returned a few moments later, "Do you think that any of these will do?" he asked, holding up an apple, a couple of cabbages and a large cauliflower.

"Perfect!" laughed Alex, adding, "You can be Vegetable United and I'll be Applepool!"

By the time Farriner and Slipp returned to the yard, the two boys had been joined by a couple of Tom's friends and were running around like headless chickens, chasing a large green object that rolled unevenly in front of them.

There were fruit pieces and vegetable bits everywhere as the two men pulled

up in the cart, the horse gratefully eating anything it could find on the ground.

When the boys saw the cart return, they stopped, kicked away what was left

of the cabbage they'd been playing with and ran to greet them.

"Is all well, Father?" asked Tom, helping Farriner down from the cab seat with

a sticky hand.

Farriner grinned broadly. "Yes, Teagh was especially pleased to see us. Sir

Granville-Greville and his staff were delighted too, saying that the King and

his guests are most excited to try our wares."

"Especially all our new 'Arabian dishes!'" Slipp winked at Alex.

Just then, Georgie appeared in the yard, looking more than a little flustered.

"Excellent, just in time. Supper's on the table. It's a good job that Hannah

and I didn't wait for you two to come to help us, especially as Alice has failed

to show her face either! She said crossly, looking at Alex and Tom, who

looked at one another, giggling sheepishly, much to Georgie's annoyance.

"I'll have to have words with that maid of mine in the morning, she's next to

useless. Can't rely on her to do anything!" Farriner barked, "Do your friends

want to stay for supper?" he asked Tom, gesturing with his head behind him

at the other boys who stood in the yard with them.

Tom turned and looked at his friends, who were obviously brothers, judging by

the ginger hair and freckles they both shared. They shook their heads back at

him.

"Thank you kindly, but we have to be off home now," said the taller boy, his

brother nodding in agreement, "Shall we meet with you and play again on the

morrow, Tom?"

Tom nodded enthusiastically. "Yes, and be sure to bring some more friends with you, Ned. Let's make a real game of it!"

Ned beamed. "All right then. Me and Harry had best be going, farewell." And with that, the two boys raced off, kicking an apple down the street in front of them as they ran.

Tom and Alex watched them disappear between the houses before following everyone else back into the bakery.

What they found as they entered the room took their breath away. Spread out before them, covering the table, were various pastries, loaves of bread, pizzas, pasties, cheeses, meats, fruits, vegetables and the biggest pork pie Alex had ever seen in his life! He felt like he must have died and gone to food heaven, such was his excitement.

"Well don't just stand there," exclaimed Hannah, "get stuck in!" No one needed a second invitation and they all began to tuck in with great gusto. Food and drink flew about them as they bit, tore, ripped, chewed and swallowed their way through everything on offer.

Gizmo had carefully positioned himself in the perfect position under the table, running back and forth, gathering up in his mouth any food that fell on the floor from the table above, like a furry little vacuum cleaner!

Farriner took a large bite out of what almost looked like a ham, mushroom and tomato pizza. "Hmm, most agreeable!" he said, tomato sauce dripping down his chin, "I think that you may have happened upon a winner with your peetzers, Master Slipp!"

"I think that you might just be right!" chuckled Slipp, taking a huge gulp of drink from a goblet in front of him. He smacked his lips together loudly, looking at Farriner, who, in turn, raised his own goblet back at him.

"Thought that you'd like a drop of the real stuff!" he winked as Slipp took an even bigger mouthful of the Mead he'd been poured

"Bleeeeeeeeeeeeeeeech!" he burped loudly, "Oh dear! Please excuse me? Where are my manners?!"

Hannah laughed and shook her head. "There's no need to apologise Master Slipp," Hannah said,   "Belching is considered to be a good way of showing that you have enjoyed your food."

Alex and Georgie looked at each other. "Great!" Said Georgie, "Buuuuuuuuuuuuuuuuuurp!"

"You sound like a bullfrog! Paaaaaaaaaaaaaaaaaaaarp!" giggled Alex, joining in the game.

"Stoppit, stoppit," roared Tom, rolling about on the floor, "I think my sides are going to split!!"

"Hrrrrrrrrrrrrrrrrrrrrrrrrrrrrrrrrrrrrumph!!!"

Everyone suddenly stopped and looked at each other.

"That didn't sound like a burp at all," Georgie said, sniffing the air, "that sounded more like a far-"

"Urgh! That's disgusting, smells like someone's pooed themselves!" Alex interrupted, almost gagging as he spoke, "Who on Earth did that?"

Everyone looked at each another, suspiciously, as they all, in turn, shook their heads. Slipp bent down and looked under the table at Gizmo, who was sniffing the ground where he sat!   "He who smelt it, dealt it," laughed Slipp as

Gizmo ran out from under the table, as though trying to get away from the stink bomb his bottom had created.

"You have one incredibly smelly cat, Master Slipp, that was truly hideous!" Worse than anything I've ever smelt in London!" Farriner laughed nasally, pinching his nose tightly," Methinks no more food for him!"

After finishing their mini-banquet, everyone sat together around the table, tired and full, but contented. It was Slipp who broke the comfortable silence.

"Thank you so much, I have had a most wonderful evening, I can't remember when I last laughed so much!"

"Nor I, Master Slipp, it's been good hearing such mirth echoing through our home again. It's been all too quiet since my dear wife was taken by the plague last year." Tom and Hannah both nodded sombrely, the pain of their mother's loss clear to see on their faces. Everyone fell quiet, uncertain as to what to say next.

It was Farriner himself who broke the silence, forcing himself up from the table, before satisfyingly patting his tight, round stomach. He looked over at Hannah and Georgie, who sat closely to one another.

"But, ladies, she would most definitely have approved of the spread that you prepared for us! Fit for a king, no less! Alas, however, the hour is late and I'd best be getting on."

Hannah looked pleadingly at her father. "Can it not wait 'till the morning, you look and sound most tired?"

Farriner shook his head. "'I'm afraid not my dear. I want to get a head start before tomorrow. We've won back the favour of Sir Granville- Greville with our delivery tonight, but we cannot afford to give him any opportunity to doubt us again. After all, you know what sort of man he can be when crossed!"

Slipp began to stand wearily, his knees creaking under the effort. "Then let us help you again, Master Farriner."

Farriner smiled, gently patting Slipp on the shoulder. "You've done more than enough to redeem yourself today, my friend. Rest now, you are most welcome to spend the night with us. It may be a bit cramped, but I'm sure that we can find a way to squeeze you all in."

Slipp was extremely tempted by the offer, but, looking across at the tired faces of Alex and Georgie, replied, "That's very kind of you, but I think that we'd better be getting back home. It has been a long and challenging day for us all."

Farriner smiled. "As you wish. At least allow me to fetch you a lantern to light your way back to St. George's Fields. Will you be able to find your own way back, or would that I take you there?" he asked as they began to make their way toward the bakery door.

"I think that we'll be fine on our own," Slipp replied, "You've still got work to do and we'd best not keep you any longer."

Farriner lit a lantern from one of the fires and handed it to Slipp. He shook him warmly by the hand. "It has been a pleasure meeting you, if under trying and unusual circumstances. Please drop by when next you visit London. But not in the way you did today!" he laughed.

"Indeed! Let's us hope that we meet again," Slipp replied, gripping Farriner's hand with both of his. Georgie hugged Hannah tightly and asked her to give Mary a kiss goodbye for her. Alex and Tom made their way outside and looked up at the full moon that filled the clear night sky.

"So, remember to keep practising the footy, won't you Tom?" Alex said, adding, "after all, you'll need all the help you can get!" He playfully punched Tom on the shoulder.

Tom smiled broadly. "Every chance I'll get, Alex." They turned as Slipp and Georgie came out of the bakery, Slipp holding the lantern, which shone brightly above him, Georgie carefully carrying Gizmo.

"Right then, we'd best be off. Thank you all again for your hospitality. I wish you good luck for tomorrow, and for the future!"

"And to you all," replied Farriner as he, Hannah and Tom stood and waved Slipp and the children off, the glow of the lantern lighting the yard in front of them, before turning to make their way along the now quieter streets of London.

When their light had disappeared from view, the Farriners went back inside. "Father," Hannah said, "it is so very late. Let's us all turn in for the night. You've both had such a long and busy day. Rise early in the morning and continue then. Please." Farriner looked at Tom's tired and drawn face before nodding.

"Yes, Hannah, you're right," he replied, stifling a yawn in doing so, "There's nothing that can't really wait until then." Farriner placed a hand gently on Tom's shoulders. "Get you to bed, Tom. We have an early start in the morning," he said, drawing a large bolt across the bakery door.

"Goodnight Father," Tom replied, making his way tiredly up the stairs.

Farriner began to wipe the table down. "Father, to your bed now!" Hannah called sternly as she started to mount the stairs herself.

"Yes dear," Farriner chuckled, gathering up a lantern and quickly joining his daughter, "I'll ask Alice to sort out down here, useless girl!"

Neither one of them noticed one of the oven fires that still burned brightly as they turned in for the night…

The journey back to, and across, London Bridge was a far cry from earlier that day. The streets were mostly empty, with only a few people passing them by as they made their weary way back, too tired to speak more than a couple of words to one another.

It took Slipp and the children around half an hour to reach the field where they had left the Time Skipper. It then took another fifteen minutes to find the right clump of trees it was hidden behind!

Slowly, wearily, they pulled the machine out from its hiding place and found a flat area to rest it upon. Slipp carefully checked over it whilst Alex and Georgie slumped on the sofa, Gizmo curled up between them, purring softly.

"Well, everything appears to be in order," Slipp declared, walking around the television and sofa one final time, "Now, where did I put that remote control?" he asked, anxiously rummaging about under the coffee table.

"It's in your dressing gown where you left it!" yawned Georgie impatiently.

"What? Oh yes, so it is." Slipp replied, pulling it out from his pocket, dislodging a couple of carrot tops hidden in there. "Right then, let's go home!" he continued, tapping away on the keypad, "No mistakes this time. First, I'll reset all the dates to make sure that we go back to the right year. Then I'll set the time for 4 o'clock in the afternoon, well before the thunderstorm. Just to be on the safe side. That ought to give us plenty of time to put things back to normal," Slipp handed the glasses to the children, "Put these on, but only after looking back at old London for one last time," he said, sighing.

The three of them turned and knelt on the sofa, looking over the back of it in the direction of the River Thames. A plume of black smoke filled the air above the moonlit London sky, wisps of it floating across it, scarring the face of the moon.

"Look like there's a fire somewhere over there," Alex said pointing, as more smoke drifted over the houses like a large thunder cloud. Flames were now becoming more visible in the distance as the fire began to take hold.

"Yes, you're right and it looks like it is quite a serious one……wait!" Slipp exclaimed suddenly, grabbing Alex's arm, looking closely at his watch. "It couldn't be? No, it's not possible. It is! Oh, what an idiot I am!" he shouted, slapping himself repeatedly on the forehead.

Alex and Georgie looked on, scared and confused. "What? What is it?!"

Slipp slumped back down into the sofa. "Today's Saturday the 2nd of September," he said quietly, looking more tired than before.

"So?" Georgie asked again, even more confused.

Slipp sighed and shook his head sadly. "Don't they teach you anything in schools nowadays? That's the day the Great Fire of London started. The 2nd September 1666. In a bakery. In Pudding Lane. London."

Alex and Georgie's mouths dropped open, their eyes like saucers. "NO! You don't mean…?"

Slipp nodded. "Yes, I'm afraid I do. What a fool, I should have realised. Farriner, The King's Baker. That's where it all started."

Alex and Georgie quickly got off the couch and started to run back in the direction of London Bridge. Slipp shouted after them. "Wait! Where do you think you two are going?"

The children stopped and turned. "To help them put it out. After all, we helped cause it!" Alex replied, a determined look on his face.

Slipp walked up to them and gently put his arms around them both. "No, you didn't because it's meant to be. You can't stop it from happening because it already has in our timeline. Were we to go back and change things, the history that we know would change too. London wouldn't be the wonderful city it is today if it hadn't have burned down all those years ago. We might not have ended up with a modern fire service either. You saw for yourselves that the houses were made of wood and built far too closely together. It was an accident waiting to happen. We can't change such a major turning point in our history, can we? It's an event pinned in time, one that must be left untouched. It's already happened, history tells us so."

"But what about Master Farriner? Tom, Hannah and Mary?" Asked Georgie, her eyes brimming with tears.

Slipp smiled kindly back at her. "Don't worry, the Farriners all escaped unharmed." Gently, he took them both by the hand and led the children back toward the Time Skipper. "In fact, very few people died or were hurt during the fire. Most of the damage done was to the houses and buildings. Some people believe that the fire helped get rid of the disease known as the Black Death, a plague that killed thousands of people in 1665, including Master Farriner's wife. So, please try not to worry, it will be all right, trust me!"

Alex and Georgie nodded sadly as they continued to look at the red glow that was filling much more of the skyline than before, causing London to look more like a fireplace than a city.

"Come on now children, it's time to go." Reluctantly, Alex and Georgie followed Slipp back to the sofa to prepare for the journey home.

The three of them tiredly buckled their safety belts, Georgie picking up the sleeping Gizmo and gently tucking him under her belt. The children then put on their dark glasses, the burning city reflecting in them briefly before pitching their eyes into darkness. Slipp rested his own glasses on the top of his head as he pointed the remote at the Black Box.

"Hometime," he said as he again checked the date, just to be certain, before tapping '1-6-0-0' on the keys of the remote control. He paused briefly, then pressed the ENTER button firmly, quickly sliding the glasses down to cover his eyes. The black control box whirred into life.

As before, after a moment of silence, a loud whirring sound began as the display's numbers flashed once, then twice, changing from red, to amber, to green. A moment or two later, the lights stopped flashing, followed by the high-pitched beeping that signalled that their journey was over.

They all sat perfectly still for a couple of minutes, scarcely breathing, not daring to move. Finally, Slipp took off his glasses, his eyes still tightly shut. Slowly, he opened one eye, then the other and, peeping round the sofa, gave out a loud sigh of relief. "It's all right guys, we're back, safe and sound."

There they were, sat again in Slipp's living room, as they had all done what seemed like a lifetime ago.

"YES!" shouted Alex as he leapt from the sofa, grabbing his cousin and hugging her tightly, without meeting any protest from her, relief overwhelming him. He let go of her abruptly and looked down at his watch.

"We've done it, it's 4 o'clock again!"

"Great! That means that my Dad's computer should be okay as well then!" Georgie said, as first, she hugged Slipp, who seemed slightly taken aback by the gesture, and then her cousin. "Thank you so much, Lord Slipp!" she cried happily.

Slipp smiled broadly. "You are most welcome. Anytime!" he laughed, winking, "Apologies for the slight detour we took, but we got here in the end!"

"Yes, we did! Well, we'd better be going now, but we'll see you again, soon!" Alex said as he and Georgie began to head towards the front door, "That's a promise!"

"I shall look forward to it!" Slipp called after them as he watched Alex and Georgie run down the drive, dodging the puddles on their way.

As soon as they got back to Georgie's home, they ran straight up the stairs and into her Dad's office. There, strewn everywhere, were the papers and files as he had left them earlier that day, before the two of them had started the chain of events that led them to London in 1666. Georgie sighed with relief, then turned to go back downstairs. "Aren't you gonna turn the computer on and make doubly sure that it's ok?" Alex asked as he followed her.

"I never want to touch that blooming computer again!" she snorted as they continued down the stairs. When they reached the hallway at the bottom, Alex turned to Georgie and gave her another hug.

"I think that I am going to go home now, and go straight to bed!" he announced, turning the handle on the front door.

Georgie looked at him and shook her head in disbelief. "But it's the middle of the afternoon!"

Alex grinned. "True, it is now, but remember, we've also spent an entire day in London today too, haven't we? I'm absolutely shattered!"

Georgie let out a large yawn, stretching her arms out wide as she did so. "Come to think of it, so am I. I'll see you tomorrow, Alex!" She said, kissing him on the cheek.

For once, Alex didn't wipe it away. "Ya big soppy girl!" he chuckled, setting off down the garden path as he began to make his back home.

When he got there, Alex went straight upstairs to bed and, without even bothering to change into his pyjamas, was asleep as soon as his head hit the pillow. So heavily did he sleep that he never heard his Mum return from her marathon shopping spree. Nor did he hear his Dad stomping through the house in his brand new, limited edition, Space Wars anti-gravity boots, which didn't work of course! He didn't even hear his parents talking to each other in the doorway, saying how cute he looked when asleep, and sucking his thumb as he did when a baby, a habit that they thought he'd grown out of.

Alex just slept, as he'd never slept before, not even stirring when his parents changed him into his pyjamas, before tucking him safely under the duvet.

Chapter 9 – Home Sweet Home?

It took everything that she could do for his mum to wake Alex the next morning. "Alex, wakey, wakey, sleepyhead! It's gone 12 o'clock! You'll miss the game at this rate. With a start, Alex sat bolt upright and rubbed his eyes vigorously, his hair sticking up at right angles all over his head.

"Really? Sorry I've lost all track of time," he yawned, drowsily.

His mother smiled and, licking her fingers, tried to flatten his wild hair down.

"Sleepyhead," she repeated lovingly, "you look like you haven't slept in a hundred years!"

"If only you knew the half of it Mum!" he whispered, hugging her tightly. "If only you knew."

"Come on then," smiled his mum, "just this once, you can have your dinner in front of the telly with your Dad." Alex nodded enthusiastically and, putting on his dressing gown and slippers, followed her down the stairs.

His Dad was already sat on the sofa in front of the television, his feet on a footstool in front of him. He patted the seat so that Alex could sit beside him. Alex looked at the sofa, then the telly, and sat in an armchair in the corner of the room instead.

"Dad, if you don't mind, I've had enough of sofas for a little while!" Alex said.

His Dad, looking a little puzzled, smiled. "Of course I don't mind son," he replied, shrugging his shoulders and turning his gaze back to the television.

"Can you turn the sound up a bit please?" his Dad added, pointing to the remote control that rested on the arm of Alex's chair. Alex looked at the

remote, then got up and pressed the volume control button on the television

instead, before sitting back down again. Instantly, the sound of a crowd loudly

roaring filled the room.

"Welcome to the spectacular Pudding Lane Stadium for today's foodball

match between two of London's oldest sides, Vegetable United and

Applepool!" the commentator announced as two teams, one dressed in white,

the other in red, strode out of a tunnel into a large open air arena. The crowd

were cheering wildly all around them, holding up large banners and waving

flags and scarves around their heads.

"Come on you Reds!" Alex's Dad shouted as the teams walked across the

brilliant white, artificial pitch, which resembled a huge stone yard, with two

goals painted on the walls at either end of it. Different zones were marked out

all over the ground, with large numbers displayed in them. Alex rubbed his

eyes and squinted at the television, scarcely believing what he was seeing.

"Seriously, a Foodball match?!" Alex screamed loudly. His Dad looked at him

as if he'd gone totally mad.

"Yes, what else would it be?" he asked, looking back at the television, where

the two captains were now shaking hands in the centre zone, stood next to a

referee, who then tossed a buttered piece of bread into the air. It landed,

butter side down on the pitch.

"The winners will go through to the next round of the Farriner's Peetzers

Foodball Cup, where Sheffield Turnips await them, with a victory here today!"

continued the commentator, "It appears that United have won the bread toss

and have chosen to use melons during the first half. This gives them a slight advantage as Applepool will not be able to play with their cabbages until the second half when it could already be too late!"

Laid out on either side of the pitch, in front of the advertising hoardings, were a whole load of cabbages and melons. Dressed in yellow and crouched in between the produce were various people acting as ball boys, poised and ready to throw the fruit and veg into play whenever needed.

"Remember, there must be a winner here today, so if the scores are level after extra time, then we'll have a sudden death Pomegranate shootout!" the commentator added excitedly.

Alex sat open mouthed and watched in amazement as the white team kicked off, the melon sailing high into the air, before exploding on top of one of the red players as he tried to head it away! The referee blew his whistle, another melon was thrown onto the pitch and play continued. Pieces of melon and pips flew everywhere, covering all the players, the pitch and the crowd! Players jostled, punched, pushed and pulled each other, running back and forth, kicking food everywhere. Alex continued to watch silently, before suddenly jumping up and running out of the room. He grabbed the phone from the side in the hallway and dialled Georgie's parents' number. It seemed to ring forever.

"Hello, Aunt Flora, is Georgie there please?" he asked urgently when the phone was finally answered.

"Georgie, are you up yet?" bellowed Flora. Alex could just about hear Georgie shout back angrily. "She's coming sweetheart," Flora continued, whispering, "but mind what you say to her. She's a right moody badger when she first wakes up! Here she is now."

"What do you want?" Georgie said grumpily as she snatched the phone out of her mum's hand.

"Georgie, something's gone terribly wrong! We've changed history somehow, we've got to go back! There's no football anymore, it's foodball! They play with melons and cabbages now!!" Alex cried desperately.

Georgie started laughing hysterically. "Well, that's no big loss, is it? Stupid flipping game anyway, perhaps it will be more fun to watch now that they're playing with fruit and veg!"

"No, no don't you see? It's because of me! I showed Tom how to play football with an orange. Then we played with his friends, who must have told their friends and they then must have told their friends, and made teams! Now it's called Foodball! It's wrong! So wrong! We've got to go back and sort it out, put it right again!" Alex pleaded.

"If you think that I am going to go through all that nonsense again just for a lousy game of football," argued Georgie, turning to look out of her hall window, "then you've got an...." she stopped mid-sentence.

"I've got a what, Georgie?" Alex asked. Silence. "Georgie?"

The phone remained quiet for a moment before Georgie's voice came through again, but only as a whisper from the other end of the line. "I think that Foodball's the last thing we need worry about. Go and look out of a window. Now."

Alex walked into the kitchen and peered out of the window. His eyes bulged at what he saw. "Oh my god!" he gulped, "What have we done?"

"I really don't know," answered Georgie, "but we are going to have to do something after all! I'll meet you at Slipp's house. He's the only one who can help us all now." And with that, Georgie hung up, leaving Alex alone with his thoughts and the dialling tone.

"Time to go then," he muttered to himself as he put the phone back down on the hall table, opened the front door and ran outside in his dressing gown, pyjamas and slippers. Back toward the lone house on the hill, back into history, back into time, onto their next adventure.

What did Alex and Georgie see that chilled them to the bone? Can Slipp help

them put history right again? Will Applepool beat Vegetable United?

And just how smelly is Gizmo the cat!

Find out when our heroes return in their next exciting adventure.

SLIPP SLIDING AWAY

Slipp Sliding Away

Slipp, Alex and Georgie are back! Literally! Our misadventurers are back home. Back in Codswallop. Back from 1666. Back to the present day. But home is a whole different world now from the one that they left just twenty-four hours before.

Returning to school after the summer holidays, Alex and Georgie are shocked to find that all that they once believed is no more, replaced by an alternative history dominated by a name from the past, of a man that they had briefly encountered before.

Discovering that they may be directly responsible for this strange, new world, the children have no choice but to ask again for help from their kind, but eccentric, inventor friend to right the wrongs caused by their actions. Using his not-so- technical no-how, Slipp has now modified the Time Skipper to help take them back to the exactly the same time and place in the past where fate intervened to change the future.

But a careless mistake and a simple coincidence disrupts their plans as they find themselves pitched into the middle of a deadly argument between two powerful and ambitious men who hold the fate of a kingdom in their hands…

Printed in Great Britain
by Amazon